**W9-ATX-973**

# BLACK STAR,
# BRIGHT DAWN

# BLACK STAR, BRIGHT DAWN

**Scott O'Dell**

Houghton Mifflin Company
Boston   1988

*Library of Congress Cataloging-in-Publication Data*

O'Dell, Scott
  Black Star, Bright Dawn.

  Summary: Bright Dawn must face the challenge
of the Iditarod dog sled race alone when her
father is injured.
  1. Iditarod Trail Sled Dog Race, Alaska —
Juvenile fiction.   2. Eskimos — Juvenile
fiction.   3. Indians of North America — Juvenile
fiction.   [1. Iditarod Trail Sled Dog Race,
Alaska — Fiction.   2. Sled dog racing — Fiction.
3. Eskimos — Fiction.   4. Indians of North
America — Fiction]   I. Title.
PZ7.0237Bm   1988       [Fic]       87-35351
ISBN 0-395-47778-6

Printed in the United States of America

P  10  9  8  7  6  5  4  3  2  1

This story is dedicated to the brave legions of mushers, women and men, who have run the Iditarod, the grueling dog sled race across two vast mountain ranges and the Yukon River, against fifty-mile-an-hour blizzards, in temperatures of sixty degrees below, for more than a thousand miles, from Anchorage on the Gulf of Alaska to Nome on the icebound Bering Sea. And to the magnificent dogs who pulled their sleds.

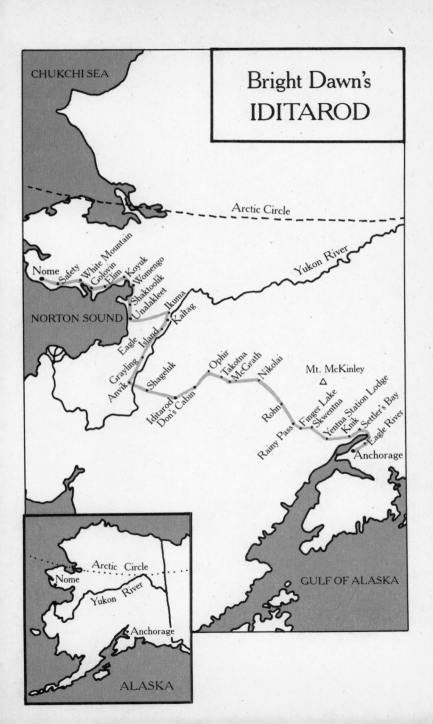

CHUKCHI SEA

Bright Dawn's
IDITAROD

Arctic Circle

Yukon River

Nome  Safety  White Mountain
Golovin  Elim  Koyuk  Womengo
Shaktoolik
NORTON SOUND  Unalakleet  Ikuma
Kaltag

Eagle Island

Grayling  Shageluk  Ophir
Anvik  Takotna  McGrath  Nikolai
Iditarod  Don's Cabin

Mt. McKinley
△

Yentna Station Lodge
Settler's Bay
Rohn  Finger Lake  Knik  Eagle River
Rainy Pass  Skwentna
Anchorage

GULF OF ALASKA

Arctic  Circle
Nome
Yukon  River

Anchorage

ALASKA

# BLACK STAR,
# BRIGHT DAWN

# 1

On the tenth day of November the sun did not rise. This was the day the sea froze up and there were no more waves. All the birds, except the ravens, flew south and we would not see them again until spring. It was very cold. The air was so still you could hear people talking far away at the end of the village.

My father did not go out on the ice that day. It was thick enough to hold a man's weight, but he waited two days, then three, hoping that leads, streaks of open water, would appear. This is the best time to hunt in the kayak, the little canoe made of deerskin.

After the third day and the streaks of open water had not appeared, a blizzard blew from the north and lasted for almost a week. It brought floating ice down from the Bering Sea, and the polar ice pounded against the ice along the shore.

1

Bartok, my father, decided not to wait for the leads to open. He told me to get the dog sled and harness the dogs. He would hunt without a kayak.

"We'll hunt bearded seals on the ice," he said.

Bearded seals are heavy. They can weigh six hundred pounds. I harnessed our seven dogs to the sled and chose Black Star to lead the team. Bartok did not like him. When Black Star was a year old, my father decided that he would never in this world make a good leader.

"He's stubborn," my father said. "You tell him something and he does something else."

"He's smart," I said, remembering the winter when we were coming home and, just on the other side of Salmon Creek, Black Star pulled up and wouldn't move. My father took the whip to him and still he wouldn't move. Then my father walked out on the frozen creek and fell through the ice up to his neck. I remembered this time but said nothing about it. "Black Star knows a lot," I said.

"Of the wrong things," Bartok said. "He's got too much wolf in him. His father came from Baffin Bay and had a lot of wolf blood. They bred him to a Siberian husky. So he's mostly wolf."

I liked Black Star. I had liked him since he was a month old. There were seven in the litter and he was the most playful of them all. He bounced around and took nothing from his brothers and sisters, giving two bites for every one he got.

He was of the purest white, with a black star on his forehead and black slashes under big eyes. But of everything, it was his eyes themselves that captured me.

They were ice blue, the color of the ice that floats down from the Bering Sea on the days when the sun is at its tallest. At first I thought how cold and suspicious and wild they were, looking at me from a world I had never seen and would never know.

After a while, I felt that behind this look was a shadow of friendship. That changed and I saw nothing but friendliness. Then that changed, too. Sometimes, when moon shadows were on the trail and we were hauling things down from the forest, the wild look would come back again.

Before I harnessed him to the sled, Black Star went down the gang line, his bushy tail curled over his back. His ears pricked forward. I had seen a motion picture one time at school about a parade in Washington. There were soldiers standing in a line and a captain walking along, stopping to look at each one of them. Black Star reminded me of the captain, only when he stopped, he reached out and gave the dogs a sharp bite on the ear.

"I tried hard to break him of that," my father said.

"He wants the team to know that he's the leader."

"Yes, but they know he's the leader without having their ears bitten off. Maybe you can do something with him."

"I'll try," but I liked Black Star the way he was.

"You could harness him up first. That way he won't have a chance to go along biting ears."

"You tried that once, remember? And it didn't work at all."

"I don't remember."

My father could forget something he didn't wish to remember. Now he didn't want to remember that he had used a whip on Black Star. He was a strong-willed man, but the dog was strong-willed, too. He was silent as Black Star went down the line biting ears, all the while watching the caribou whip.

"There isn't a cloud in the sky. What a fine day to hunt," I said.

Last winter my father had killed only three bearded seals and there was a whole month when we didn't have much to eat. Hunting would be better this year, my father said. He was good at telling how far south the seals would go on their summer travels — a thousand or two thousand miles — and when they would return to the cold waters of Womengo.

The full moon was rising. There were scratchy clouds far down in the west, but it would be a fine

4

day. Bartok got out his hunting things, put them on the sled, and got in beside them.

"We hunted the south shore last year. Bad luck," he said. "Maybe we should hunt north this year. What do you think?"

"North," I said, eager to go in any direction.

My mother took her time to answer. She was wearing a parka she had made in the summer of fox fur and wolverine. She looked very pretty.

"South was bad hunting last year," she said, handing Bartok some smoked salmon strips to eat while he was out on the ice. "So it should not be bad this year again."

"No, I am sure," Bartok said. "Last night I had a strange dream. I was gathering clams along the shore. Out of the sea came a bearded seal. He was very thin and could barely move on his flippers.

"'I have come a long way,' he said. 'I am starving. Will you give me some of your clams?'

"I was about to say that I needed them for my family. Then I saw that each of his ears was a gleaming pearl. At once, I knew that it was the King of the Bearded Seals.

"'You can have all of the clams — there are more than two dozen — if you make me a promise,' I said.

"'I am starving. I'll promise anything, Bartok Machina.' (He knew me, he called my true name.)

5

"'Then promise that you'll have some of your subjects, many of them, visit our shore this winter.'

"'A hundred. Two hundred.'

"With that, he scooped up the clams, swallowed them in one gulp, and waddled fast into the sea."

Every year this sort of talk went on between him and my mother, Mary K. When he went out on the ice they would always talk this way and always about a dream he'd had.

There was a reason for such talk. Hunting is dangerous. Danger lurks everywhere. Killer whales are thirty feet long, and if a man is hunting in a kayak they can snatch him up, kayak and all. If it's angry, a Kodiak bear can kill a hunter with a single swipe of its paw. Polar bears are the worst of all. They feed on seals, and because hunters always smell of seals, the bears think they are seals and track them down. A hunter does not go out on the ice without fear. But he is not a man unless he does go.

Women never hunt. My father was even criticized for letting me drive his sled to the ice, to help him bring back the seals he took. Women's place was at home.

I had been doing it now for two winters. It started when my brother was killed on the ice, the day he speared a bearded seal with the harpoon rope looped around his neck and was dragged into the depths and drowned. In my father's eyes, somehow I became his son who had died on the ice.

The hunters in the village and their wives did not like me to go out with my father. It made no difference to him. For a long time now I had driven the sled to the ice and helped him load the heavy seals on the sled, and driven back home. Often we drove down the village street in broad daylight so everyone could see us.

# 2

Smoke from breakfast fires hung above the village. Men were starting off toward the south. My father and I went north. We went along the shore, hunting for a good place to go out on the sea.

During the freeze-up, polar ice was driven down through the Bering Strait by north winds and struck the shore. The collision flung up great mounds and spires and ridges, mixed with sand and rock. These *eewoonucks* formed an icy wilderness between the shore and the frozen sea.

It took us nearly an hour to find a place to hunt. We staked out the dogs and climbed a jagged ridge. My father saw the head of a bearded seal, just the top of it, sticking up through the ice. The seal sank out of sight when it saw us.

My father climbed down from the ridge and gathered up his things — his knife and his harpoon with the long rope fastened to it. He followed the ridge until he came close to the stretch of flat ice and the breathing hole where the seal had shown its head.

Between my father and the hole was a narrow bridge of ice. He got down on his hands and knees and crawled slowly from one side to the other. Seals have good ears. They can hear footsteps many yards away through the ice.

I watched him crawl to the lip of the breathing hole and not move for a while. He coiled the long rope harpoon. Then he crouched beside the hole a step away, his legs braced, his body bent forward, and the harpoon in his hand.

My father was the best hunter in our village. It was because he was very patient. He could crouch for hours this way, bent over, waiting for a seal to show its head. Often he waited for half a day, sometimes for a whole day, and when I brought him food he wouldn't eat it for fear he would not be ready with the harpoon.

There was so much waiting that I always brought schoolbooks to read. In this way I was able to keep up with my studies. My teacher, Helen Tarrana, was good about letting me make up the time I lost. But today it was so cold, the pages wanted to stick together. I did manage to read about the golden seal, which does not inhabit our waters. Her fur jacket is made of hairs so fine that three hundred thousand are packed into one square inch so that she's always warm and waterproof.

9

Imagine! Who counted all these hairs? I wondered.

Books can be exciting, useful too. My mother named me out of a book she was reading the morning of the night I was born. It was about seals, the beautiful creatures who live in two worlds. She came to a place in the book where, in the deepest of a sunless winter, for some strange reason, a day dawned bright, bright as a day in spring. That is how I got the name. Bright Dawn.

I closed my book, climbed down from the ridge, and fed the dogs, who were restless. Then I climbed back up and kept an eye on my father. He had not moved. He looked like an ice statue crouching there among the *eewoonucks*.

The moon was full. By late morning its light began to fade. A south wind came up and shifted around to the north. It was much colder now. I climbed down and built a fire and warmed myself. Then I climbed back up the ridge. Bartok still hadn't changed his position beside the breathing hole.

The seal had another hole somewhere, I decided. Seals can't stay down for much more than five minutes before they have to come up for air.

The wind died and it started to snow, large flakes at first, then small ones that had ice on the edges. We were miles from home. Part of the distance was through the *eewoonucks*. I called to my

10

father to give up the hunt. He did not answer. By now he looked like a snowman.

I called again. Slowly he raised a hand to quiet me. The snow was coming down harder, but it was very still, except that from far off I heard the rumbling of shelf ice.

I climbed down from the ridge, taking my time. It was very slippery. The dogs were lumps in the snow. I scraped them off, searched around for driftwood, and tried to build up the fire. I had no watch, but I was good at telling the time of day. It must be an hour after noon, I decided.

The fire would not burn and from a cloudy sky the moon cast only weak shadows. But I found my way along the path Bartok had taken. It was hard to see. I got down on my hands and knees and crawled to the edge of the shelf and groped along to the bridge that connected the shelf to the polar ice.

It was not there. Instead, I saw a jagged point sticking up like a spear. Beyond, I caught a glimpse of blue water, the sea.

I cupped my hands and shouted. The wind flung the shout back in my face. Was my father on a floe that was drifting away from the shore? Had he come back to the bridge, found it gone, and taken another way to reach the shore? Wherever he was, I would never find him.

I went back to the camp, harnessed the dogs,

and started off against the raging wind. The *ee-woonucks* all looked alike. I did not try to find the way back to shore. Knowing that I would never find it, I walked along beside Black Star and let him guide us.

When we were near home, Mary K. heard us and was at the door. She was calm. Mothers and wives were always calm when bad news came. They were trained to hear bad news. Not a winter went by that at least one of our men was not lost on the ice.

Mary K. hurried into her parka. My feet were wet, beginning to freeze, so I changed my socks and boots and we ran up the road, spreading the news through the village. All the women and the old men came out and followed us to the outpost store.

Anvo Noorvik, the man who owned the store, said, "Nothing can be done until the hunters come in from the ice."

We knew that.

He looked at his watch. "Six o'clock," he announced. "Some will be back in an hour. Everyone will be back in two hours. In two hours we will start the search. Now we will return to what we were doing."

When we came in, Noorvik was opening a box with a pry bar. The bar was still in his hand. He gave the box a jab as we filed out.

Everyone wanted to take us into their homes, but my mother refused. We walked into the blizzard, heading along against it, through the village to our home. But we felt better, having been with our friends.

# 3

The first thing I did when we got home was to tie a leather rope across the room under the ceiling.

If a rope goes limp, my father had told me, it's a sign that the hunter is in danger. If it goes limp more than a little, if it hangs down, then the hunter is dead. Then the clothes that hang behind the stove to warm him when he comes in are taken down and put away forever.

An hour went by. The rope did not move. The blizzard piled snow against the windows. It shut out the light, so I lit candles. My mother busied herself over the stove. She did not believe in the rope. She had gone to a school in Nome where they did not like what they called Eskimo superstitions.

When we heard dogs barking in the village, I ran outside and started toward the store. The blizzard was at my back and I went fast.

Most of the men were home from the ice, more

14

than twenty of them. They had heard the news from Anvo Noorvik, but they wanted to know it from me. I told them what had happened, leaving out nothing that I thought would help. They hugged the hot stove and were silent. I wondered if they would ever thaw out and talk.

At last, squat, lank-haired Utak Tuktu, who was a good hunter, said, "Now we go to look for Bartok."

"To find him," Louis Katchatag said.

"And bring Bartok home," someone said. "He is safe. He is friends with the ice for a long time."

I asked Tuktu if I could go with him. He didn't bother to answer.

Hunting on the ice was not something for girls or women. This I knew well, but I asked him again as the men filed out. Again, he didn't bother to answer.

They took four dog sleds and nine kayaks. I followed them down the road and saw them disappear in the driving snow.

When I got home, my mother was watching the deerskin rope, even though she said she didn't believe in it. "It hasn't moved a bit," she said. "It still hangs tight."

We cooked supper and ate some of it. The blizzard had stopped. I cleaned the snow off the window so we could keep track of the weather. The moon shone in a cloudless sky.

Around midnight we heard dogs barking in the village. I went up the road to see what it was. The last of the hunters were returning from the ice with the seals they had killed.

We divided the time; my mother slept for an hour, then I slept. Toward morning, while I was watching the deerskin rope, I saw it move, or thought I did. I got my mother and she sat down and watched, too.

"I see nothing," she said, a little angry with me for believing. "You are tired. Your eyes are tired."

"They are not tired," I said, begging her pardon.

We watched together for a while. Then I got up and made breakfast, a big one, pan bread and all. Ten long hours and more had passed since the men had gone out. My father could be coming home now.

An hour past noon a sled came up from the south. I ran out, thinking it might be a sled bringing my father home, but it went on to the village. When I got there, they were carrying Louis Katchatag into the store. He had fallen into open water and was covered with thick ice, even his face.

After he was thawed out, Katchatag told us that my father had been sighted. He was on a large ice floe moving slowly north past the village. The hunters thought they could reach him in a few hours if the wind didn't move the ice floe away from the shore.

I went home and told my mother what I had heard. It was good news, but she said nothing, getting up to look out the window, coming back to keep an eye on the deerskin rope.

Neighbors brought food, special food like caribou steak, that they knew Bartok liked.

The wind came up and slapped hard against the house, against one wall, then another. We couldn't tell what direction it was blowing from. It blew cold air down the chimney and filled the room with so much smoke that we couldn't see the stretched rope.

I got out a pair of my father's best mukluks, the ones made from sealskin bleached in winter weather, soft and almost white. I had made the tops. They had patterns of different-color fur and bands of wolf fish skin. They looked fancy.

Boots are as good as ropes for telling how things are.

I hung them up by the window, where I could see them clearly in the moonlight. As long as the boots move, even a little, if they walk, the hunter is alive. If they stop walking, the hunter will never, ever wear them again in this life.

Hunters drove by on sleds and went to the store to thaw out and eat. I cooked food for them. All the women cooked food. The men were hungry. Jack Eagle ate three thick caribou steaks and a loaf of bread before he went back to the ice.

The news was good. Whenever the snow let up they had caught glimpses of my father. He was still on the big floe and it was moving along the shore, not out to sea. That day, if they could steer a kayak through the fields of floating ice — they had lost five kayaks already — they would reach the floe and bring my father home.

# 4

Late that night, we heard sleds on the road far to the south. They came closer, passed our house, and we ran after them.

The hunters carried my father into the store. He was stretched out on one of the kayaks. They put him down by the fire and covered him with a robe. He said nothing.

"He's doing pretty good," Anvo Noorvik said. "But he's got a bad hand. It's frozen. Turning black. He needs a doctor."

There was a heavy silence while Anvo Noorvik went into his office and started up his radio. Crackling sounds and sputtering voices were all we heard for what seemed like an hour. It could have been half an hour.

I stood beside my father. He was under a mound of fur robes and I couldn't see any part of him. I spoke to him and he said a few words that I didn't understand. They sounded as though they came up out of a deep hole.

Anvo Noorvik said, "I got Doc Evans. He's over in Grassy Creek working on broken legs. He'll be here in six hours or less, depending on the weather."

John Evans was the only doctor between Womengo and Nome. He traveled around, making regular calls at fishing villages along the Sound. Dr. Evans had saved many lives.

Driving his team of six malamutes, he reached the store at gray dawn and operated on my father. He had to take off all the fingers on Bartok's right hand, all except his thumb.

"Your husband is a strong man," Dr. Evans said to my mother as he left to go up the Sound to Ovakoff. "The worst is over."

We took my father home, but the worst was not over. His hand healed, but there was something strange about him.

About two weeks later, I was sitting by the window, working on the sealskin boots I sold to people in Nome who sold them to visitors in the summer. Our house was on the shore and the window faced westward to the sea.

My father glanced out at the jumbled spires of the *eewoonucks*. With a groan, he yanked the curtain shut, plunging the room into darkness.

I got up and lit a lamp. As I walked back to the

table where I was working, the light shone in my father's face. His eyes were two deep hollows. His mouth was twisted to one side. His bronze skin was pale underneath. For a moment I thought I was looking at a ghost.

That day he ate little of the food we cooked for him. That night I heard him talking in his sleep. I could not make out what he was saying, though it was loud, so fearsome that the sled dogs on the porch stopped their singing. They did not raise their voices again that night.

My father was the chief man of our village. He was called *an-yai-yu-kok*, the one that everyone listens to. Everyone did listen to him. But two days later, on the morning the elders met to talk about problems, he did not appear. They thought he had forgotten to come, so they sent a messenger to our home to remind him.

When the messenger knocked on our door, my father did not answer. He sent me, saying, "Tell them that Bartok has a fever in his head."

He was silent. He sat all day with his back to the window and stared and said nothing. Whenever the big ice floes drifted down from the north and crashed onshore, making thunderous sounds, he would tremble and turn pale.

Early in February the elders decided that the village should have a new *an-yai-yu-kok*. My father hadn't been to the meetings for a long while. They

21

chose a new man whom everyone listened to, but said nothing to Bartok about it.

Then Dr. Evans came on one of his visits to the village. He was surprised at what we told him. How my father had quit going to the council meetings, that he never left the house, that he kept the window closed and sat with his back to it, how he trembled whenever sounds drifted in from the frozen sea.

Dr. Evans motioned for Mother and me to go outside. It was a warm day and he stood in the yard with the hood of his parka thrown back. He was tall and broad-shouldered and towered over us.

In a doctor's voice, he said, "I have seen a dozen cases like this before. Hunters who were caught on floating ice and drifted for days, for a week, not knowing at what hour they would freeze to death, afraid to sleep for fear they will not wake up. Others who fell into the sea by accident, who would have died in minutes from the cold had they not been rescued. Not one of these men ever hunted again. It's a phobia."

The sled dogs were barking, eager to be back on the trail. Suddenly they were silent. Bartok had come out to the shed and was listening to us.

My mother had never heard the word "phobia" before. I could tell that it startled her. I had heard it used in school about mad animals, but it startled me, too.

22

"Fear," Dr. Evans said, "is powerful."

"My husband has hunted since he was a boy," my mother said. "He is not a fearful man."

"Deep down, all hunters are fearful," the doctor said. "But your husband is fearful now, every minute of his life."

"What will happen? What can we do?" my mother said.

"Hard as it may be, it's best that you leave the village and go where this man cannot hear or look at the sea or even smell it. I know of a place. Ikuma. It is on the big river, where fishing and hunting are good. Ikuma has a good school, a better school than here. I am going there next week. I will find you a place to live."

My father came out of the shed huddled up in his parka and turned away from the sea, blinking in the wan light, smiling a wan smile.

Three days later we moved to Ikuma, forty miles from the seacoast. We hadn't much to move — the pot-bellied stove, cooking pans, dishes, knives and forks, a barrel of smoked salmon, a barrel of seal meat, and the six caribou skins we slept on.

We piled everything on the big sled and Bartok drove. He stood straight on the runners. He looked almost the way he did before those days on the floating ice. The dogs were eager to go.

Mary K. and I got on the sled and covered ourselves with one of the caribou skins. My father cracked his whip. It curled around the dogs' ears. When we came to the hill that looks down on our village, my mother glanced back.

"Bartok was born in Womengo," she said quietly. "And his mother and father were born in Womengo. Their mothers and fathers were born in Womengo. It is sad that we will not see our village ever again."

"You will like the new place," I said, though I felt sad, too, and I had no idea what the new place would be like.

My father cracked his long whip again. He shouted at the dogs and did not look back at the village or the frozen sea.

# 5

Ikuma was not a village like Womengo. It had more than a thousand people, a post office, two cafés, and three stores besides a trading post.  .

At first, we lived on the far side of the river, at the edge of the tundra, a great treeless place. Our makeshift house was made of birches bent over and tied at the tops and covered with caribou skins. After a year, after my father got well and found work with the Empire Canning Company, we moved to a house in town and I had my own room, the first one I'd ever had.

The school was much bigger than the school in Womengo. There were three teachers. Helen Grammas taught English and history, such as the Constitution and the Revolutionary War. Ellen Dusek taught arithmetic. John Seward taught geography and other things.

There was also a church where the Reverend Cartwright told us about God and the Devil, about heaven and hellfire. I got mixed up listening to him, because I had always believed in the God Sila.

Sila is a mystery. He lives far apart from us, way off in nothingness. No one has ever seen him. No one has ever heard him speak. But he watches to see that we do not harm the world we live in — the air and water, our friends the animals, the land and the sky. If we do harm them he will become angry and all of us will vanish from the earth like mist in the morning.

John Seward encouraged us to play games. He led the school band and taught me to play the trumpet. Dog sledding was a very popular sport. The school had two sleds, three dogs to the sled, and he taught us how to race. He could do everything.

The Yukon is a wonderful river for sleds. It winds back and forth like a mammoth snake. And in places it is more than a mile wide. When the ice is covered with a light snow and the dogs can get a footing, the sleds fly.

I was the only student in school who owned a dog team, but in the town there were dozens, and most of them raced on Saturdays.

Usually the races were thirty miles long. The prizes were merchandise from the stores and meals at the two cafés. I never won, but I did finish every race and came in second twice. I won a dinner at the Blue Goose Café and once a glass cooking dish.

My father didn't like his job at the Empire Canning Company. They canned salmon in the spring, but this was deep winter. The big tin building was deserted. All Bartok had to do was to be a watchman for three hours, six days a week, and look out for prowlers. It was a lonely job, walking around empty tables and silent machinery. When he got home, he never had much to say.

"Why don't you go out like Bright Dawn does and race the dogs?" Mother asked him one night.

My father frowned. "Dogs are meant for work, not for racing."

"They are trained to do both," I said.

He gave the supper table a blow with his big fists. They set the dishes to rattling. "For work, not for play," he said.

But we kept at him. Every night at supper we brought up dog sled racing. It took us most of the winter to get him on a sled. We were not surprised that he came in third in his first race and won a pair of beaded mukluks. In the next race he came in first and won a new parka.

After that he was on the river every Saturday and I didn't have a chance to race until spring. He was very short and had a bow in both his legs, but he was strong. In the bad places he jumped off the sled and pushed and kept pushing for an hour, even with his bad hand. He grasped the caribou whip with only his thumb and sent it singing along

27

the backs of our seven sled dogs. He won six races, then the big one, the three-hundred-mile race, and $500.

Ikuma was a check station on the Iditarod, the famous dog sled race that starts in Anchorage on the Gulf of Alaska, crosses rivers, vast stretches of frozen tundra, two great mountain ranges, and ends in Nome, on the Bering Sea, after 1,179 perilous miles.

At Ikuma, drivers check in and out. Their times are kept in a book and sent by radio from one checkpoint to the next. In that way it is known which drivers are first and which are last and which in between.

The Iditarod was a big event in Ikuma, the biggest of the whole year. People talked about it months before it happened. I played a horn in the school band. Two weeks before the racers came through the town, we practiced on Yukon Street, marched up and down, and got ready to greet them.

The mushers came on the nineteenth of March. It had taken them more than thirteen days to travel from Anchorage to Ikuma. They still had to travel one hundred and seven miles to reach Nome.

The night before they came and even the night before that, I couldn't sleep. I had heard about the Iditarod for years. In Womengo people talked about it, but I never thought that I would stand in a crowd somewhere and watch the race. I had never dreamed in my wildest dreams that someday I would march in a band playing my silver horn, wearing a spring parka trimmed with wolverine fur, and welcome racers of the famous Iditarod.

It snowed hard all day on the nineteenth of March, but everyone in Ikuma was waiting on Yukon Street when our school band gathered in front of the Gem Café and welcomed the first drivers with "God Bless America" and "America the Beautiful."

Seventy-one mushers had started from Anchorage, we heard, but only thirty-five arrived in Ikuma. The rest had dropped out.

They checked in, one after the other, for three days. On the third night, the last driver that appeared was a girl. She staggered when she got off her sled. She looked so cold and bedraggled that I invited her to come home with me. She smiled weakly.

Her name was Deborah Reed. She was about nineteen, a year or two older than I, and came from Penobscot in Maine.

My mother cooked a hearty meal for her, but she didn't eat it. All she wanted to do was sleep.

"For how long?" I asked her.

"Forever," she said.

"There's hot water. Do you want a bath?"

"Sleep," she said.

"Are you going to give up?"

She thought for a moment, then shook her head.

"When do you want to leave?"

"Wake me in five hours, please."

She fell asleep in the chair. She had frostbite on her cheeks.

I went outside and fed her dogs. I kept track of the time and got her up in five hours. She ate two bowls of soup, and I made her some moose sandwiches.

"I've run in some races," I told her. "But they were nothing like the Iditarod, of course. Tell me about the Iditarod."

"You bounce along on a rough trail," she said. "Sometimes on no trail at all. A wild wind blows in your face and the temperature is forty below. With the wind, it could be one hundred below. You freeze and think you are going to die and wish you would. You sleep four hours a day. You wake up and make a fire and feed a dozen dogs. You examine their feet and legs and boots. You harness them to a towline. It snows. The snow turns into a blizzard.

"Comes another day. It's the same but different. You climb a steep hill, too steep for the dogs, so you get off the sled and push. The dogs want to lie down. You urge them on. Over the hill the trail plunges down, back and forth. You stand on the brake. You put out the snow anchor, but the sled races on while you grit your teeth. Then there's another day. The same but not the same."

Her face was pale under the skin that the cold had blackened.

The sun came up and she got on her sled. The dogs lunged against their harness. I watched her disappear in the falling snow. With all my heart, despite what she had told me, I wished I was on the sled racing for Nome.

Then something strange happened. That night while we were eating supper, Bill Weiss, president of the Empire Canning Company, and Frank Gibson, owner of the Gem Café, appeared.

"Every year," Mr. Weiss said to us, "we enter a driver in the Iditarod."

"We have entered six drivers, but none of them has won," Mr. Gibson said. "In fact, none of them has ever finished the race. It's not very good for Ikuma. Gives Ikuma a bad name."

Mr. Weiss said to my father, "We've heard about the races you've been winning around here."

"Quite a record you've established," Mr. Gibson said.

"We've been wondering if we could enter you in next year's Iditarod," Mr. Weiss said suddenly.

My father was startled.

Mr. Gibson said, "The first prize is fifty thousand dollars. There are other prizes, too. One hundred and fifty thousand in prizes."

My father was silent. Money did not mean anything to him. He thought the white man was crazy, talking money all the time. If my father could gather warm parkas for his family, boots that kept the water out, dry wood for the stove, enough seal and fish to last the winter, then he was a happy man and made us happy.

Mr. Weiss seemed to know this. He was half Eskimo and half Tlingit Indian. It was the Tlingit part that had made him rich.

"It's not the money so much," he said. "It's the test. In the Iditarod a man finds out who he is and what he is. It's a test of bravery."

My father rubbed his bad hand against his chin, a sudden glint in his eyes.

Then Frank Gibson said that they would pay for everything — supplies, food for the driver, food for the dogs, food drops at the checkpoints. "Everything. A dog team, if necessary."

"It takes a year to train for the Iditarod," Mr. Weiss said. "You'll be on the payroll of the Empire Canning Company, the same as always, but you'll spend ten hours a day on the trail, getting your team in shape."

My father was dumbfounded. He stared at the two men.

Mr. Weiss said, "You should start training tomorrow."

My father sat and stared.

# 6

Early the next morning a sled drove up in front of our house. A man with a gray beard got off the runners. He came to the door and spoke to my father.

"My name is Peter Avakoff," he said. "I've been hired to help you get ready for the Iditarod. I've raced in two of them. Came in fifth and tenth. Raced in the last one, too, but my heart acted up and I had to drop out."

My father was still recovering from the shock Mr. Weiss and Mr. Gibson had dealt him the night before.

"Are you ready?" Peter Avakoff said.

My father didn't answer. He was out the door, dragging me along. Together we harnessed up our dogs.

"I need weight," he said. "What do you weigh, Bright Dawn?"

34

"One hundred and twenty-nine pounds," I said.

"Jump in," my father said.

He sent the caribou whip snaking along the dogs' backs and we were off for the river, Peter Avakoff and his team running beside us.

We ran twenty slow miles down the river, then stopped for Peter Avakoff to rest and talk about the Iditarod, how it was different from all the other dog sled races. When we got back, he came into the house and talked again.

My father, who had never learned to write, asked me to put down everything, word for word, as Peter Avakoff talked. How to pass another team on the trail and keep your dogs from fighting the other team. How often to feed the dogs. How much — not all they could eat — and what food was best. Water was very important. How often they should drink and how much, surely not all they could.

My father had seven dogs on his team.

"You need twice that number," Peter Avakoff said. "You'll lose dogs along the way, virus and accidents. You have to finish the race with seven at least."

It took only a day for Mr. Weiss to find more good dogs, trained dogs that had raced before.

After that, the two men went out every day and four times a week at night, because a lot of the Iditarod was run at night. I went with them on Saturdays.

I took down what Peter Avakoff said. By summer I had a small book of notes. Every week my father asked me to read them over to him from the beginning.

When the ice on the big river broke up, he and Peter Avakoff took their teams into the hills north of the village, where deep snow still lay on the ground. They trained all summer, though most of the snow had melted by July, going out days and nights and traveling at least fifty miles each time.

After most of the snow had melted, there were stretches of mudholes and quivering ground that shook and bounced the sled. It wasn't much fun, but Peter Avakoff told my father that he would encounter lots of mudholes in the Iditarod and it was a good idea to get used to them.

In November, John Seward put the two dog sleds from the school together, borrowed another team from the Trading Post, and entered me and my friend Julia Englet in the three-hundred-mile Ikuma–Nome Express Race. We were out for four days and had fun but came in twenty-first and twenty-second.

It was the next month, after a heavy snow had fallen, that my father and I had the terrible accident.

Early one Sunday we were out on the trail. My

father tried to pass Peter Avakoff's team. Our sled was bouncing, and I was holding on tight with both hands. We were halfway past the other team. Our dogs were barking at his dogs. Bartok snaked out the long caribou whip.

Now we were past them. We were about to swing back onto the trail and Peter Avakoff shouted, "Good."

The dogs were kicking snow in our faces. Suddenly our sled slipped to one side of the trail, then to the other, but it didn't straighten out. It rose in the air, came down, rose again, tipped, skated along on one runner, and crashed against a tree.

My father was on his feet before I got to him. We were both dazed and covered with snow. Peter Avakoff untangled our dogs. We got the sled right side up and headed back home. Bartok made a joke about the accident, but he looked so pale that I knew he was injured.

Ikuma did not have a doctor. We had a good veterinarian, though. Dr. Goshaw looked at Bartok and took X-rays and said that his left shoulder was cracked in two places. He wound it up with yards of tape, made a sling, and gave Bartok some medicine, which he didn't take.

Mr. Weiss and Mr. Gibson came while we were eating supper. They had heard about the accident and talked to the veterinarian.

My father jumped up from the table and made

a show of being in fine shape. "Three weeks and I'll be back," he shouted.

Mr. Weiss gave him a sharp look. "That's not what we hear. The vet says you'll be laid up for six weeks, maybe longer."

Mr. Gibson said, "That's too bad."

"Terrible," Mr. Weiss said.

Both men were sympathetic, but I felt that already they had made up their minds that Bartok would not get well in time for the race.

"Three weeks and I'll be back," my father said, still shouting, swinging an arm to show them how strong he was.

"Say you are back in three weeks," Mr. Gibson said. "That will be the middle of January. The race starts early in March. Your team needs to run fifty miles a day to get in shape. That's more than a thousand miles gone, lost, down the drain."

"Bright Dawn will train the dogs for me," my father said. "She's a good trainer."

"But what if your shoulder doesn't heal in three weeks?" Mr. Weiss asked. "What if it takes six weeks? Two months, the vet says. What happens then?"

My father didn't answer.

"Well, I will tell you what happens," Mr. Weiss went on. "We've spent more than twenty thousand dollars on fees, food for you, food for the dogs, food drops here in Ikuma and other checkpoints. On the best sled money can buy. On seven trained malamutes that alone cost us forty-two hundred dollars. We've spent all that money, and there we would be on the day the race starts with no one to race. Do you get the point?"

My father sat down at the table. Then he got up and strode across the room and looked out the window at the falling snow. Then he came back and sat down again. He did not answer Mr. Weiss.

In the lamplight his cheeks had a rosy glow, but his hands, clenched in a knot, were white. He glanced at me, started to say something, and stopped.

For a long while there were no sounds in the room except the crackling of wood in the big stove.

Then Mr. Weiss said, "These are the facts, Bartok. What do you think we should do? Wait and see what happens? Gamble that you'll get well in a month or six weeks? What?"

It seemed terribly hard for my father to answer. Words came out of his mouth slowly. "My daughter will run the race," he said.

Mr. Weiss and Mr. Gibson were startled. They looked at each other, then at me.

Mr. Weiss said, "But your daughter's too young. She's still in school."

"A schoolgirl," Mr. Gibson said.

I could say nothing. I was overwhelmed by the thought of racing in the Iditarod. Then I got all of my wits together in a hurry.

"I am not a schoolgirl," I said. "I graduated from school the tenth of this month. I have a diploma. There it is on the wall."

I pointed. The men turned and glanced at the diploma.

"And I am not a girl. I'm eighteen years old. I'm a woman."

"Women have won the Iditarod. Two of them," my father said. "They weren't much older than my daughter."

"I know, I know," Mr. Weiss said.

Mr. Gibson said nothing.

They put on their parkas. As they left, Mr. Weiss said, "You will hear from us. Soon."

It was not soon. A day went by. Almost two days went by. I gave up hope on the second day, but my father told me that he had had a vision.

"They will come tonight," he said. "They have decided. You will run in the big race."

"Will I win? Will I win?"

He thought. "The vision is not clear about the winning part."

Mr. Weiss and Mr. Gibson came while we were eating supper. They took off their parkas. They stood by the stove and warmed their hands and said nothing. I poured two mugs of coffee for

40

them. They didn't thank me, they just stood there getting warm.

"What news do you bring?" my father said to the men, impatient with them.

My mother stood silently by the stove. Her hands were clasped together. From the first she hadn't liked the idea of my running in the dangerous Iditarod, though she had said nothing. She never went against my father.

"What?" he asked, raising his voice.

"Good news," Mr. Gibson said.

"Very good news," Mr. Weiss said. "I've talked to the people in Anchorage. I've given them the facts about the races your daughter has run, her age, and so forth. She is entered in the Iditarod."

"And tomorrow you start training," Mr. Gibson added.

"Tonight," I said.

Before they left, I got out the notes I had taken down from Peter Avakoff and read them over. The next morning as the moon set I was on the river with Peter Avakoff and the fourteen dogs. He sat in the sled and I drove. I had never driven more than seven dogs. The fourteen dogs seemed to stretch out in front of me for miles.

I would need to learn how to control that many dogs. It was done only by voice commands, not by reins. "Go!" "Whoa!" "Gee!" for a right turn. "Haw!" for a left turn. "Come gee! Come haw!" for a complete turn, depending on whether the turn was left or right. And shouted so the leader heard.

"Today we go five hours," Peter Avakoff said. "We go slow. We come back slow. Tomorrow the same. In a week we will choose and see who goes where in the line."

I knew half the dogs already. They were friends.

The two wheel dogs, the dogs that ran side by side directly in front of the sled, were named Thunder and Lightning. Thunder was a male malamute, gray with a black overcoat. Lightning, a female, looked much like him. They were brother and sister and ran well together.

The next four dogs in the line were from a different litter, but all had been bred by the Malamute Eskimo tribe, who live near the mouth of the Yukon River.

They were named Sun, Moon, Sky, and Blizzard. The first three were brown-eyed, tawny-colored dogs. Sun and Moon, gray Alaskan huskies, were tireless. Sky, who had some malamute and husky blood in her, was dependable. Silver-coated with an amber mask, Blizzard was different from the other six dogs. He never ran faster than he had to, but in a pinch he could fly. He was my father's favorite. He had used him as a leader and liked him better than Black Star.

Black Star, as I have said before, was *my* favorite. This morning I put him in the lead. With his tail furled and ears aslant, he seemed to enjoy being out in front of thirteen dogs, seven of them strangers he would soon lord it over.

Peter Avakoff and I raced ten hours a day for a week, and on the twenty-fifth of February I boarded the bush plane Mr. Weiss had hired to take me and the team to Anchorage. It was a holiday in Ikuma. The town came to the landing strip, the school band played, and Mr. Weiss gave a short speech.

"Bright Dawn, you will bring great honor to Ikuma. We send you away with hearts bursting with pride. We await the day when you will return to us, on your way to victory."

Victory? I was glad that he had nothing more to say about victory or about Bright Dawn, who was trembling in her mukluks.

# 7

I took a quick glance below me as the plane struggled into the air, at the world suddenly upside down. Then I closed my eyes and did not open them again until we were safe in Anchorage.

Mr. Weiss had a truck waiting for us, a huge red one with boxes for each of the dogs and a place on top for the sled. The driver took us down a street where lumps of gray snow lay melting in sunny places. The thermometer had read zero when I left Ikuma. Here it was twenty degrees above zero. I sweltered in my wolverine hat and caribou parka. The truck kicked up dust. I wondered how we could ever get out of the city on our sleds.

"You're quiet," the young man said. "You're worrying about snow. Don't worry. We'll truck snow in if we have to, all the way down Main Street from the starting line to the outskirts and beyond. You never can tell, of course. It can let loose and snow

44

three feet by morning. I hope so. We have sixty-nine racers. If it doesn't snow, we've got a lot of snow to haul."

He took us to a field where the drivers and their teams were camped. There were more dogs than I had ever seen in my life. There must have been a thousand camped in the field.

We unloaded the sleds and took the dogs out of their boxes and chained them to the truck. They set up a howl for supper. All the dogs in the field were howling for supper. They made a dreadful din.

I had a cooker that used charcoal and made a hot fire. I put charcoal in the bottom and sprinkled it with Blazo. A square pot fitted on top of the cooker and held five gallons. I put some snow in the bottom of the pot, then the frozen meat. Peter Avakoff cooked meat for exactly thirty-five minutes. I did this also. It made a fine stew. The dogs liked it, wolfed it down, and begged for more.

Now it was dark. The camp sparkled with fires. Smoke rolled through the night. Everywhere the dogs were quiet. I got into my sleeping bag and curled up on the sled. I was too excited to sleep.

There were four days more before the race began. I spent part of the time going over all the things the rules said I must carry — an ax, snowshoes, a hunting knife, a flashlight, and a sleeping bag. I had six extra batteries for my headlamp. Mr. Weiss had bought me a watch with a dial that glowed in the dark.

I saw that my clothes were all in shape. I had two parkas, a long one for the cold, a short one for when I was on foot, running with the team, and two light parka covers. I took inner and outer deerskin pants, two sealskin blouses, a pair of mukluks and a pair of softer boots to wear under them, a pair of gloves and a pair of mittens. My hood was trimmed inside with wolverine, a fur that does not freeze.

For the dogs I had more than a thousand boots to keep the snow and ice from cutting their feet. Often I had to change their boots every forty or fifty miles. The boots were tough, made of canvas and sewn with fishing line.

I had enough food to last me to the second checkpoint at Rabbit Lake, where the planes would drop more food. For the dogs, a mixture of frozen caribou and salmon in small packages that were handy to put in the cooker. For myself, corned beef hash and canned fruit. Also some Eskimo ice cream, which you make by taking reindeer tallow and a little seal oil and heating them hard, adding water and oil until everything is fluffy. Then you put in some cranberries or strawberries, any kind of berries. It is a wonderful treat. Hunters take it with them when they go out on the ice.

I noticed that some of the drivers had a mat made from automobile tread hooked to the back of their sleds. To slow the team down, you simply stood on the mat. It was better, they told me, than a brake or a hook. I found a piece of tread, made a mat out of it, and fastened it to the back.

I polished the runners and went over the gang line and all of its fastenings. The steel hooks on the brake were a little worn. I borrowed a file from a driver who was camped near me and sharpened them.

The driver was an Eskimo from Fox Island, far north of Nome. He was short and broad and when he walked he looked like a bear.

"Oteg," he said, giving his chest a thump, speaking Eskimo. "That is my name."

His eyebrows were white and his skin was the color of caribou hide. He had small black eyes that were set far back in his head. He squinted at me and I saw nothing but two black slits.

"You look like my youngest daughter," he said. "Her name was Panee. What is your name?"

"Bright Dawn," I said.

"Panee died one day long ago. Too bad. She was a pretty girl. Now I have only nine."

He counted the girls on his fingers and said their names, but I caught the name of only one of them, Nuna.

"I am an old man," Oteg said. "I give my daughters good advice. They do not listen to me. Do you listen?"

"Sometimes."

"Have you raced this race before?"

I shook my head.

"Oteg knows much about this race. I have run it three times. One time I came number twelve. One time I came ten. One time I did not finish the race. There was a moose on the trail one night near Ophir. The moose came out of the trees. It walked into my team and killed three dogs. Sad. Look for moose, they are a big danger on the trail. Moose and the times you cannot see the trail and get yourself lost."

He glanced at me out of his small black eyes to see if I was listening.

"This time I run better," he said. "Who knows? Maybe I come first." His eyes glittered. "Where will you be?"

"I don't know, but I think about it every moment."

"Think more! The race is won by thinking. Think about what you will do the first day. Will you go fast? Will you go slow?"

"My team is fast."

"Then I will give you advice. You like advice? Good. Slow the first day. Let the dogs lope. Let them walk. We draw numbers for the start. If I start first, catch up. If I start later, then I'll catch you."

It snowed hard in the night, a foot of powdery crystals.

# 8

The drawing was held three nights later. All the sled drivers were there. Drivers from the lower States, from Spain and Switzerland, from Italy and France and Canada. There were four women drivers and two girls my age.

I got number 23 to wear around my neck. Oteg got number 39. The dogs got a spot of blue paint on their backs. This was to make sure that the dogs that reached Nome would be the same ones that left Anchorage. No dogs could be added along the way.

Race day dawned bright and warm. The temperature was nearly five degrees above freezing. After their long rest, my dogs were wild to be on the trail — so wild that the handler tied his sled to mine to hold them back. Even then we crossed the starting line before we were supposed to and had to come back.

Black Star acted the worst of my dogs. He stood

on his hind legs and pawed the air. He bucked like a bronco. He yelped and barked.

I held on to the handlebar. I planted my feet on the mat. The starter counted down from ten, down to three, down to two, down to one. Yet when he shouted, "Go, driver, go!" and the dogs lunged forward, I lost my footing but held tight to the handlebar. The handler's sled slowed us.

I got back on the mat and we went slowly down the street. Crowds cheered us, and a little girl ran out and gave me a pink flower.

The drivers started two minutes apart, Oteg thirty-two minutes after I did. The trail was packed hard by the sleds in front. Four teams passed me and I passed no one. Late in the afternoon Oteg caught up with me. He was pleased.

"You listen," he said. "You are not like my nine daughters. Good!"

At five o'clock we came to the checking station at Knik. We had traveled fifty-nine miles. I was thirty-fifth and he was thirtieth among all the sixty-nine drivers.

"Good for us," Oteg said. "Tonight, tomorrow, we run where we are. The day after tomorrow we move up, to thirty and twenty-five, maybe."

A warm wind blew from the south as we left Knik. The stars sparkled in a clear sky. Near midnight, before we reached Rabbit Lake, the next checking place, I heard the sounds. I shone my

51

headlamp on Black Star to see if he had heard them, too. He always ran with his ears laid back tight to his head. They were cocked up now. He was listening. He heard the same thing I did.

I thought the sounds came from the teams ahead of us. Then they were on my left. They were softer than those moose or caribou make, more like fox or wolverine. I turned and shone my head-lamp on the back trail. The nearest team was a mile away.

There were no more sounds, but Black Star still ran with his ears cocked up, listening.

The sky clouded over. The wind shifted to the north and blew bitter cold. I put on my heavy parka and my mittens, which were warmer than my gloves. When we came to Rabbit Lake at two o'clock in the morning, many teams were already there, camped on the hillside.

After we checked in and picked up the food our plane had dropped, we traveled for half an hour and made camp.

"It's no good to stay at the check stations," Oteg said. "This way there's no fighting among the teams and so the dogs get more rest."

I staked out the team and cooked them their supper of meat and salmon. Oteg shared his supper with me. It was a string of herring eggs and six candlefish the size of my little finger. The wind blew hard and was very cold.

I asked him if he had heard animals stalking us before we came to Rabbit Lake. "They could have been wolves. But I never saw them."

"No, you can't see the wind," Oteg said. "The wind has no head and no body. Only a voice."

"I heard the sounds."

"So did I. It was King Raven! He has disguised himself and become the wind. He wishes to cause us trouble."

Oteg went to his sled and came back with a handful of small, sharp knives. They were carved from yellow walrus tusk and tied in a bunch with sinew. I had seen their like before. They were called "weather cutters." Many people in Ikuma owned them and believed that they could change the weather by cutting it into pieces, just as they wished it to be.

Oteg did a dance in the snow. He shook the bundle of knives above his head and muttered, "Wind, who blows cold from the north, we've had enough of you. We do not wish to freeze and soon we must travel fast. Speak to your sister, South Wind. See that she replies."

Sleds were passing us. We harnessed the team and set off on the trail to Skwentna. Before we had gone far, the wind that had buffeted us during the night died away. Near dawn, in the darkest of the night, I heard the sounds once more.

At dawn, while we were moving amid tangled

brush, I caught a glimpse of animals traveling. It was a pack of wolves. The leader was white with dark yellow markings on his face.

Suddenly Black Star brought the team to a halt. I shouted, "Go!" He did not move. I walked down the line of dogs and shouted again. Still he did not move. He threw his head back and closed his eyes. A chill sound came from his throat. It was not one sound but many. It was the sound of ice breaking up on the big river. It was the sound the sea makes in an angry storm. It was like the sound the little snow owl makes on a wintry night.

The leader of the wolves answered him. The two howled together. The sounds became one. They rose and fell, rose and fell. Then they trailed off to a whisper.

I waited. The wolf leader moved away. Then I heard him no longer. Black Star fell silent. I scolded him and he scolded me back. Then I bent down and put my nose against his to show him that we were still friends.

Oteg said, "Raven was the wind. Now he has changed. Now he is the leader of the wolves. He has many faces. But I know his tricks. I have a charm against them."

He reached in a pouch he wore at the end of a string and took out an amulet of blue beads and heron feathers. He rubbed it between his palms and muttered a few words, which I did not understand.

"Have no fear," he said. "Now King Raven will not follow us."

When I was a child I heard about King Raven. How we people were only specks of dust until he came. How he picked up a speck of dust and rolled it hard on his black tongue and dropped it into the sea. After that, many people and animals appeared.

Among the animals were two beautiful wolf-dogs. They roamed the hills. They fed upon fat rabbits and drank sweet water from the rivers. They were very happy until Raven, the jealous trickster, came and gave them a burdensome task. He commanded them to sit on a lonely rock by the shore. He told them to bark loudly twice each day and make the tide flee. Thus, every day the sea has two low tides, forever.

"King Raven is trying to lure the dogs," Oteg said. "He will fail."

I did not believe much in Raven and his power, though more than the Reverend Cartwright thought I did. But from that moment I kept an eye on Black Star in the daytime and always at night.

# 9

We came to Skwentna early in the morning. We had run a hundred and forty-eight miles from Anchorage. I was still thirty-fifth and Oteg thirtieth.

Teams were camped everywhere in the icy meadow. Blue smoke drifted up from their fires. An airplane landed and brought food for us and the other teams.

We went on for half an hour and camped until four o'clock in the afternoon, then we left for Finger Lake. It was two hours after midnight when we got there. Our places in the race had not changed.

Oteg said, "We will sleep until we have good daylight. Rainy Pass Lodge is the next station. The trail twists like a snake. It goes down and down and back and forth. It is the most dangerous part of the trail. You can go over the bluff and fall into Happy River Gorge. We go rapidly until we get there."

"Good," I said. "I am tired of poking along."

We started with Oteg in front. My dogs were eager to run and I let them. We caught up in a few minutes and passed him. It was wonderful to hear the runners sing, to feel the rush of the wind, to see the trail skim by and the dogs running with their ears laid back.

Before I got to the bluff, a sled came up fast behind me. It was number 41, the girl I had talked to the morning the race began. Her name was Katy Logan and she lived in Ohio.

She had a team of pure white Samoyeds, fifteen of them. Samoyeds are dogs raised in Asia to round up reindeer. She shouted "Trail!" in a haughty voice, and I moved over as much as I could to let her pass. She was soon out of sight.

At the bluff I took Oteg's advice and slowed down. Snow began to fall. It hid the tracks of the drivers in front of me — also, the trail the snowmobiles had cleared out for us. The red metal stakes that marked the trail were far apart and some had fallen down.

I rode with one foot on the mat and the other dragging in the snow. Still, we went much faster than I wanted to.

As we rounded the second steep turn in the trail, suddenly I came upon a sled lying on its side. The dogs were tangled in their harness.

I jumped off and shouted "Whoa!" at Black Star,

but our heavy sled ground on. As I passed the wreck, as the girl stared helplessly at me, Black Star veered off the trail and brought us to a halt against a snowbank.

We were on the very edge of the bluff. I looked straight down and saw the banks of the frozen river. Black Star glanced back at me and wagged his bushy tail. He was proud of himself. I told him what a fine dog he was.

The girl was covered with snow. Her frozen pig-tails stuck out like sticks. She had rolled up the sleeve of her parka and was rubbing a swollen arm. Her dogs were trying to free themselves from their tangled harness. She was too dazed to help them. After I straightened out her team, I went over to the sled, which was teetering on the edge of the bluff.

Her sled weighed no more than thirty pounds, a beautiful racer barely two feet wide and six feet long. It had a fold-down seat over the runners. I picked it up and set it on the trail. The carriage had broken, but both runners were in good shape.

Oteg rounded the steep turn, singing at the top of his big voice, and pulled up behind me. He was not surprised to see the pile-up. He took it in at a glance.

"No time for talk," he said. "You go with your dogs," he said to the girl and to me, "You go next. We'll talk later at Rainy Pass."

We started down the gorge and passed an abandoned sled but no driver or dogs. The snow was falling harder than before.

In the middle of the afternoon we came to Rainy Pass Lodge, having covered seventy-four miles from Finger Lake, two hundred and nineteen miles since we left Anchorage. We were running twenty-first and twenty-second in the race.

Oteg said, "We will feed the dogs now and rest until night comes. If the snow stops, we go. Night is best for traveling."

# 10

It stopped snowing, but we did not go. The marshal "froze" the race. No one was allowed to move. A radio message from Rohn, the next checkpoint, said that the weather was so bad, planes could not fly in with food.

We had a hard time finding a place to camp. The fields were covered with staked-out teams. Before we did find a place, word came that the "freeze" would last for at least two days. Oteg found a place on the riverbank among some stunted spruce trees.

He cut a hole in the ice near the riverbank and caught eight big trout, more than enough for the dogs and our supper. The fish turned hard as wood the instant the cold wind struck them. Oteg hacked them up into pieces and I put them in the cooker.

"We will be here for two days. Maybe three, who knows?" he said. "It is best to build a snowhouse."

"I will not be here," Katy Logan said. "I am going home."

"Too bad," Oteg said.

He picked out a flat place under the trees and we scraped off all the new snow, down to the snow that was old and packed hard. "Now we get out the knives and cut some blocks," he said. "About two feet one way and two feet the other way. Square."

Katy Logan was nursing her swollen arm, but she got out a knife. I had helped to make an igloo at school, so I showed her how to cut the blocks. I handed them to Oteg and he put them side by side in a circle. When he had one row, he trimmed off the top edges so that each of the blocks slanted in.

We worked until there was a circle three rows high. It was not yet an igloo, but it helped to shield us from the bitter wind. After we fed the dogs and cooked the trout, we put our sleeping bags inside the circle, got into them, and went to sleep. Before morning we were three mounds of snow.

At dawn we began again on the igloo. One by one Oteg added rows of blocks until they met above the top. He got down on his knees, cut a round hole in the wall, and crawled out. The cracks between the blocks were filled with soft snow. The opening at the top of the dome was closed with a piece of clear ice.

We finished at dusk. Oteg caught more trout. I fed the dogs and cooked supper, which we ate in our igloo. It was below zero outside and above zero inside our new house. I was warm for the first time since I left Anchorage.

The wind blew in wild gusts. It smashed against the snowbank that had piled up outside. Then it rumbled over the igloo's dome and shrieked away into the night.

"The wind cannot get hold of the roof. It is too slippery," Oteg said. "Igloos are very good in the wind. They are good all the time except in the summer, when they melt and fall on your head. If we stay here another day and night we will build a porch for ourselves, a very good place to cook in."

Katy Logan asked, "Our friend keeps saying *na-ma-kto*. What does it mean?"

"*Na-ma-kto* means 'very good,'" I said.

Oteg had brought a lamp with him and set it up between us. It was not really a lamp, simply a hollowed-out piece of soapstone. Filled with chunks of frozen seal and fitted with a long cotton wick, it glowed and made blue shadows dance against the walls. I should have felt snug but I didn't. I wanted to be on the trail.

I had not seen or heard the wolves again since the night we were near Skwentna. I did not hear them now. Black Star was tied tightly to a tree, but I brought him inside the snowhouse. He lay quietly beside me except when the wind moaned. Then he raised his head and pricked his ears.

"It is very good to have the dog here," Oteg said. "No rope will hold him with Raven prowling about."

Katy Logan asked what Oteg was talking about. When I told her, she said, "Do you believe all that stuff about Raven?"

"Not when the sun is shining," I said. "But on nights like this, I wonder."

Somehow Oteg got Katy Logan's sled through the door. He took off the handlebar. Then he began to wrap the sinew around the places where the sled was broken.

The wind had shifted from north to east and blew harder now in gusts.

"With Raven about, we are lucky to have such a strong snowhouse," Oteg said. "I feel sorry for this Raven sometimes. I remember what a poor beginning this fellow had. At first, when he was only a speck of dust and people were only stones, he was the smallest bird that ever lived. Believe me, he was no bigger than a melon seed and he had a voice like a small mosquito."

I translated everything Oteg said.

"One day the Great Spirit visited the earth to look at the creatures he had created. Walking through a village at evening time, he heard people singing the sunset song. The trees were filled with birds of every color, but none of them were singing. All were silent, listening to the sunset song.

"'Why do the birds not sing?' the Great Spirit asked.

"'Because they have no voices,' the people said.

"'What a terrible mistake,' the Great Spirit said.

"At once he called all the birds together. Hundreds, thousands of them came from everywhere. They darkened the sky. They made thunder with their beating wings.

"'At dawn,' he said to them, 'you are to fly as high as you can. When you reach the limits of your strength, then you will find your voice. The bird who flies the highest will find the most beautiful voice in the world and return to earth to sing the most beautiful songs.'

"Raven, who was no bigger than a mosquito and sang like a mosquito, knew that he had no chance to fly high, so he thought of a scheme. He hid himself in Eagle's tail. Eagle flew higher than any of the birds. But just as the Great Spirit was about to give him the most beautiful voice in the world, Raven crawled out of his tailfeathers and flew even higher. Then something awful happened that he had not imagined."

The lamp began to sputter. Oteg put in two chunks of frozen seal. Then he put a big handful of tea leaves in a pot and began to work on the sled again.

"What about Raven?" I asked him. "You were saying that something awful happened to him."

64

"Oh, yes, it was awful. When he got back to earth, he found out that the Great Spirit had watched him all the time. He had seen Raven crawl into Eagle's tailfeathers.

"'Raven,' the Great Spirit said, 'you are a cheat. So therefore I will not give you the most beautiful voice in the world. Instead, your voice will be the worst, caw, caw, caw.'"

Oteg poured tea for us. It was so black and bitter I couldn't get it down. He drank mine, then three cups more, then ate the tea leaves. Then he smacked his lips and looked content. I wondered if he had come to race the Iditarod or just to tell stories and have a good time.

It stopped snowing during the night and the gray dawn was quiet. But drifts were piled high against the doorway. Katy Logan and Oteg were fast asleep. I had to dig a tunnel to get out of the igloo and attend to the dogs.

They were buried in the snow. Just their noses showed. I dug them out, walked them around, and fed them. By that time Oteg was up. He looked at the clear sky.

"Very good," he said, smiling.

After he had fed his team and I had fed Katy Logan's, we went to the station. The drivers were voting whether to stay or leave. There was a blizzard in Rohn, the next station, the radio said.

The vote was divided. Half of the drivers, of

65

those still left in the race, voted to stay and half voted to leave.

Oteg voted to stay. "This is no time to head off in a blizzard," he said to me. "The race has just started. We do not need trouble now. We have a long way yet to go."

I could see what he wanted to do. He wanted to build a porch on the snowhouse. He wanted to tell stories, burn his big lamp, brew his bitter tea and drink five or six mugs, then eat the black leaves. I voted to go on to Rohn. He was angry and muttered something about me and his daughters.

The marshal decided to hold the drivers until nightfall. But at noon an airplane came in from Nome with word that the weather had cleared ahead, and the marshal sent the drivers off. The airplane was going to Anchorage. Oteg and I helped Katy Logan get herself and her dogs on board. When he picked up her sled, she told him to keep it. "I will never use it again," she said. "It's yours."

We carried the sled back to the igloo.

"Get on," Oteg told me. "Sit on the seat and try the brake."

I tried it and put one hand on the bar and one foot on the snow. I sat on the folding seat. I stood on the runners and pretended that I was driving a team of barking dogs.

66

"What do you think?" Oteg said. "Do you like the new sled?"

"I like it. The dogs will like it, too. They'll think they are pulling a baby carriage."

The trail to Rohn was very narrow. An avalanche might slide down at any time. The marshal sent us on a new trail that led through Ptarmigan Pass.

We had lost nearly an hour helping Katy Logan. "We are far behind," I said to Oteg. "Now I am going fast and pass."

"It is a good day not to pass."

"Why have a fast sled and go slow?"

"Everyone will be running fast today. They'll be making up for the freeze. They'll wear their dogs out."

I didn't take his advice. He started off first at six miles an hour. I went twice that speed and passed him before we reached the top of Ptarmigan. He was not pleased with me, but I was tired of wandering along.

# 11

The trail through Ptarmigan was steep. The new sled flew like a frightened bird. At the bottom of the pass, just as I skimmed out of a grove of spruce trees, I saw something strange on the trail.

Snow was falling, and at first I thought it was a pile of rocks covered by brush. As I drew closer, the rocks turned into trees, then into a shaggy beast. I thought it was a caribou. Then I saw the spreading horns and the long lumpy nose. It was a moose, a bull moose, big and red-eyed.

Moose are always dangerous. They are big and bad-tempered. Oteg was far behind, and if I waited for him to come and help me I would lose all the time I had gained.

I did not dare to challenge the beast. Once when I was with my father we met a young bull near Blue Goose Village. It was standing in the middle of the trail, swinging its head back and forth.

"It does not wish to move," Bartok said.

"I don't blame him," I said. "The trail is easier to walk on than deep snow."

"And what's more, it is not going to move. It weighs most of seven hundred pounds, so we are not going to make him move."

"We can try."

"Remember old Ekaluk? He tried one time and lost three of his dogs and came close to losing his life. I have my gun, but since my eyes went bad I am a poor shot. If I only wound the beast, it will come at us."

He unhitched Black Star and the rest of the team. He turned the sled around, hitched up the dogs again, and we went back, nearly out of sight, and waited. We waited for most of an hour, until the beast decided to move away.

What had happened to Ekaluk I did not want to happen to me. Oteg had good advice about passing dog teams but not about passing a moose. I stepped down on the brake and shouted "Whoa" to Black Star. When the team came to a halt, I was so close to the animal I could hear it breathing. Its head was lowered and it stared at me with its yellow eyes.

Quietly I put on my snowshoes. I made a half circle around the moose, leaving a trail in the snow that was deep enough to run on. The dogs were barking, straining at their leashes in a frenzy to get at the beast. They did not budge when I yelled

"Go!" I had to crack the long, black whip over their heads before they would take the trail. They barked until the moose was out of sight behind us.

It stopped snowing and a weak sun came out, but the wind still blew hard from the north. I passed two teams camped beside the trail. Close to dusk I came upon a third team. The driver was pulled up behind some trees, feeding his dogs.

He raised a hand and shouted, "Watch for moose. Two big ones just trotted by." He pointed down the trail to Rohn. "I'd wait, young lady. You can get into trouble," he shouted.

"I just passed one," I shouted back, thinking that he was not warning me but trying to slow me down.

But in a short time, as the trail climbed a hill and went down again over a bridge and frozen stream, I saw the moose, the ones the driver had warned me about. There were two of them, as he had said, a bull and a cow. The bull was big. Each of my dogs weighed over seventy pounds. The bull looked bigger than all of them put together.

When she heard the dogs bark, the cow took to the stream and disappeared. But the bull stood sideways on the bridge and did not move. I pulled up the team as soon as I was sure that he meant to stay there.

Off to the right of the bridge were patches of earth and rocks where the wind had swept the snow clean. I shouted "Gee!" for right turns, then "Haw!" for left turns, and Black Star picked his way through the clean patches.

When we were safely on the trail again I glanced back at the bull. He had moved from the bridge. He was slowly trotting after us, swinging his head from side to side. I cracked the whip and the team leaped forward. But as we picked up speed, the bull did not stop, and I saw that he was chasing us.

In a long run my dogs could outdistance him — they can cover close to twenty miles in an hour — but in a short run moose could run much faster. They run at a gallop, thrusting their thin legs ahead of their bodies, two powerful legs at a time.

I was scared. I jumped off the sled to make it easier for the dogs. The moose rushed up and ran beside me. For a moment I thought he was showing off, playing some sort of a wild game. Then he ran past me and galloped along the line of dogs, brushing them off the trail with his broad antlers.

He galloped on and disappeared over the brow of the hill. My dogs were barking, trying to get out of their harness to chase him, so I waited for a while to calm them down and let the bull gallop out of sight.

But when we started up again and came to the brow of the hill, he was waiting. He stood in the middle of the trail, his long, queer-shaped nose raised to the wind and his yellow eyes fixed on us.

We were in a draw with boulders on both sides of the trail. There was no way to get around the beast, but room to turn back. I made the turn and waited beyond the hill for Oteg, for one of the drivers, for help to come.

No sooner had I calmed the dogs again than the bull appeared on the brow of the hill.

He stood for a moment looking down at us, pawing the snow. With one sweep of his antlers he could kill half the team. With his sharp hoofs he could injure the rest.

I did a desperate thing. As the bull started toward us, I ran down the towline, loosened the buckles, and freed all of the dogs. It was better that they run or hide, to save themselves as best they could, than to be caught tied to a towline.

Black Star raised his head, growled, and moved slowly up the rise to meet the bull. The rest of the dogs followed. The sled was small protection, yet I stood behind it. Not long before I had felt the biting wind. I felt it no longer.

Black Star circled the bull once, twice, three times, drawing closer each time. On the last circle the beast caught him a glancing blow with one of its back hoofs and sent him sprawling.

Black Star shook the snow out of his eyes, got up, and stalked the bull again. Now all of my dogs sent up chilling howls and joined him.

72

The bull snorted, made sounds like far-off thunder, and slashed out with his sharp hoofs. He moved round and round. He tried to face all the dogs at once but failed. Then he made a dash for Sky and gave her a slashing blow with both of his front hoofs.

I took off my parka, ran up the trail, and waved it frantically — a foolish thing to do, yet it saved us. The moose forgot he was surrounded by growling dogs.

For a moment his blazing eyes examined me and the parka. In that brief time, Black Star sunk his teeth into the beast's throat. In a flash the other dogs were on him.

The moose fell to his knees and rolled over. He tried to shed the dogs, but they clung to him until he lay still.

I wrapped Sky in my heavy parka and laid her on the sled. She was scarcely breathing. I rounded up the dogs and fastened them to the towline and started for Rohn. It was getting dark. The trail was hard to see, but I turned on my headlamp and went fast.

# 12

It was past three in the morning when I came to Rohn. A north wind was blowing. I anchored the sled and took Sky in my arms. She seemed better. But when I got her to the cabin — this was all of Rohn, a cabin beside the trail — and the veterinarian looked at her, he said that she had three broken ribs. He gave her something and she went to sleep.

Oteg came in more than an hour after I did. He had lost the trail out of Ptarmigan and ended up in a swamp.

"How many teams did you pass?" he asked.

"Four."

He clapped his hands. "Pass four today. I stay close. No more swamps. We push the leaders, not too fast, not too slow. To the others we give serious thoughts. And all the time we keep the dogs strong. Dogs win the races."

I told him about the moose.

"They are worse than blizzards," he said. "And the trails you cannot find in the snow. Holes in the ice and swamps. Moose are the worst. But today you need not worry about them. I will speak to my friend, the Raven."

A big fire was going in the cabin. He shouldered his way through the crowd of mushers, warmed his hands at the fire, and went outside. When he came back, he said that he had spoken a few words to Raven.

The stars were dim and there was a small moon. I cooked food for the team, staked it out away from the other teams, and changed the boots on all the dogs that needed them. Then I crawled into the sleeping bag, slept until dawn, and went to see about my injured dog.

She was awake but did not want the fish I brought her or any of the meat the plane had dropped or the rice and blueberry cakes I had stored away for myself.

"Do you want to *go*?" I said in the voice I used on the trail.

She cocked her ears. She looked up at me for a moment, then closed her eyes.

The morning had dawned clear and cold. I could hear the drivers talking to their dogs. The first teams were leaving. Oteg came in and wanted to know if I was ready.

"Twelve teams have gone," he said. "I am hitched. But still you moon over the dog." He was angry.

I said nothing and went out and told the marshal that I wanted to send my dog back to Anchorage. He said a plane was due.

"When?" I asked.

"In an hour, depending on the wind."

Oteg had followed me. He guessed that I meant to wait and put my dog on the plane.

"You do not win races this way," he said. "Maybe the plane comes in an hour. Maybe in two hours. Maybe tomorrow. Who knows?"

The marshal said, "The veterinarian will take care of your dog. And I'll see that she gets on the plane."

I thanked him and said I would wait for the plane. He gave me a quick glance and shook his head. Silently, Oteg left the cabin. I heard him shouting at his dogs, the crack of his whip, and the squeal of the runners.

The plane landed in less than an hour. I wrapped Sky in a blanket, Mr. McCall gave her a pill, and I put her on the plane.

"Will they take care of Sky when she gets to Anchorage?" I asked him.

"She'll have a better time than pulling a sled."

Mr. McCall did not know that she would rather pull a sled than eat.

76

I got the rest of the team ready and we left before noon. The sky was gray, but it had stopped snowing. I caught up with Oteg. He pulled off the trail so I could pass. He had gotten over his anger and shouted more advice. I did not listen. He had taught me many things about the race. But it was Oteg who was racing in the Iditarod, not me.

I remembered my father's words. He said, "Do not depend on other people, on me, on your teachers in school, on anybody. Listen and think about what you hear, but depend upon yourself." From now on I would try not to depend upon Oteg so much.

It seemed strange driving the team without Sky. The team missed her, too. She sang a lot even when we were going uphill and the snow was deep.

The afternoon turned cold. Sharp pebbles covered the trail. They were hard on the dogs' feet. I stopped twice to feed them bits of frozen meat and change their boots.

At dusk I came to the Farewell Burn. Oteg had told me about the Farewell Burn. It was thousands of acres that a fire had swept through. Stumps of burned trees rose everywhere along the trail. A thin sheet of snow covered them like shrouds. In the dim light they looked like rows of ghostly heads.

Oteg had warned me to go slow through the Burn, to watch closely for stumps. Instead, now that I was running the race in my own way, I drove faster than I should have. I hit one of the stumps and broke off pieces of both of the runners. I drove slower after that and Oteg passed me.

I got to Nikolai, the next checkpoint, at two in the morning, almost an hour after he did. It was blowing again. The wind turned into a blizzard. The thermometer fell way below zero. You could not see beyond your feet. A "freeze" was called, and not a team stirred that day.

During this time Oteg built another igloo. Or, rather, we built it together. This time, at his prompting, I stood inside. He handed me the blocks of snow and I put them down in a circle and slanted the edges to make the dome. It was not so good as the igloo we had made at Rainy Pass, but it kept out the fierce wind.

The "freeze" helped. I could not race on broken runners. New ones were not to be found in Nikolai, but Oteg poked through his bundles and found two lengths of spruce, which he fitted to the runners and bound with caribou sinew.

"I will now make the runners smooth, both of them," he said. "Now you will fly!"

He took out a blob of frozen mud and heated it over the lamp. When it was soft, he went outside and smeared it over the runners and let it freeze again. With his knife he trimmed the mud smooth. Last, he filled his mouth with water and let it warm. Then he moved up and down the over-turned sled with a piece of wet deerskin, spraying and wiping the runners. They froze in a second.

"Try it now," he said.

I put my hand on the sled and it moved easily.

"Try one finger."

I touched a finger to the sled. It glided away.

*"Aiee, aiee,"* he crowed. "When we leave Nikolai we will go a little faster than before. We will pass some teams this time."

I nodded and thanked him for saving the sled.

Just before dawn, at a lull in the screaming wind, I heard the wolf sounds again, the sounds I had heard at Skwentna.

I went outside. All of the dogs except Black Star were buried in the snow. He was on his feet, sniffing the air. His head was turned toward a grove of trees. Beyond the trees, through the driving ice and snow, I made out the white wolf. He was standing with his pack, bunched together. They were watching us and not making a sound.

Black Star was chained to the towline. I untied the chain, led him into the igloo, and set the snow blocks in place. For a short time I dozed and woke to find him clawing at the doorway. I sat up and listened.

The wolves had come closer. They seemed to be just outside the igloo, among the sleeping dogs.

Oteg crawled out of his bag. He put a chunk of

seal oil in the lamp and set water to boil for his black tea.

"The wolves are outside," I said.

"I have heard them," Oteg said. "They are looking for food. They'll find none and go away."

"It's the same wolf pack I saw before. The leader is white. He's the one I saw at Skwentna. He's not just looking for food."

"You saw the white one?"

"This morning."

Oteg sighed. "It's Raven again. I'll attend to him after a while."

He put on his boots. He poured himself a mug of tea. He drank it and poured more. Then he got into his big parka and left the igloo. He was gone for a long time. I went outside, holding Black Star on his chain. Day was breaking.

Oteg stood with his mug of tea, looking at the sky. "It's very good," he said.

The sky was pink in the east. Bands of lavender shifted back and forth overhead, faded out, and returned in shades of orange and yellow.

"Where are the wolves?" I asked him.

He had forgotten about the wolves. He sipped his tea and gazed at the beautiful sky.

"The wolves," I said. "What happened to them?"

He drank his tea and kept admiring the sky.

# 13

We left Nikolai the next morning when the sun came up and got to McGrath at dusk. We camped there past midnight, looked after the dogs, slept some, and started off for Tokotna and Ophir and Iditarod.

Oteg said, "The driver who gets to Iditarod first wins two thousand dollars in silver money. That is a good prize, two thousand dollars. But I cannot win. I am too far back. Let the others scramble and wear out their dogs, is what I think. What do you think?"

It was the only time he had ever asked my opinion about anything.

"The new sled flies. The dogs are fine. Two thousand dollars is a lot of money, Mr. Oteg. I am going to try for it."

"Well . . ." He was disappointed, but he gave me a thin smile and wished me luck.

The dogs strained at their traces. They started

off with a mighty rush. The runners sang. It was a dark night. Not a star showed. Far in the west a pale moon went down. I passed six teams on the way to Tokotna, on the way to Ophir, eight teams. Now I was running ninth.

Beyond Ophir, the mushers ahead of me had stopped at a checkpoint called Don's Cabin. Warm lights shone through the window and I heard loud voices and laughter. It was very cold outside, but as soon as I checked in, I climbed back on the sled and headed down the trail for Iditarod.

We all had left Ophir according to the times we got there, also our places in the race. At every checkpoint, these staggered starts were used. In this way every musher could keep the advantage he or she had earned.

The country beyond Don's Cabin looked wild and forsaken. Scattered trees were ragged and bent over by the fierce winds. It was very cold. My feet stuck to the runners. They felt as if they belonged to somebody else.

I drove the team faster than I ever had before. At times we were running at fifteen miles an hour. The dogs opened their jaws and scooped up snow as they ran. I stopped and fed them snacks often enough to keep them happy.

No one was ahead of me. Not one of the eight drivers I had left at Don's Cabin had overtaken me.

Yet I had no idea how much time I had gained on them or where I stood now in the race. Surely I was close to second or third.

Iditarod is a ghost town, just a few shacks left over from the gold rush, when ten thousand people lived there. As I drove in and put on the brakes, sending up a shower of snow, a marshal came out to greet me. He looked at his watch, put down figures in a book, and talked to people.

There was a long wait. Then a man came out and said, "Congratulations. You are the first driver to reach Iditarod. You are the winner of two thousand dollars."

I couldn't be the winner, but here I was. I felt giddy in the head. I had never earned more than fifty dollars making and selling mukluks. I tried to say a little speech. All I could say was, "Thank you."

The race was not over. As soon as I could leave politely, I thanked everybody again and left. I was tired and the dogs were tired, too tired to go faster than three miles an hour.

The trail wound through steep hills, straight up and straight down. Going up, I had to get off and push hard on the sled to help the dogs. Going down, I had to press hard on the brake and the rubber mat. Twice I put out the snow hook. Once I ran off the trail. Then the sled turned over and I lost nearly an hour.

Oteg caught up with me and helped to set it back on the trail and get the dogs' harness straightened out. Seven teams passed me before Oteg came.

I was glad to reach Shageluk, a village on the Innoko River. School was out, and a band of children and their teacher came and asked if I would like to take a bath in the schoolhouse. I hadn't had a bath since I left Anchorage. It was a wonderful invitation, but then I thought how awful it would be to have to crawl back into my half-frozen clothes. Then I changed my mind and used up all of the school's hot water.

Oteg didn't believe in baths. "Water," he said, "is bad. It washes you away, bits at a time. Not good."

While I was getting into warm clothes, he cooked soup for the dogs and caribou steaks for us which he bought from a villager. It was the first real food I had eaten in days. I was so tired that I had eaten only chocolate bars, five or six of them every day, and spoonfuls of Eskimo ice cream.

After Shageluk it got very cold, much below zero. My eyelashes gathered frost. They began to feel like splinters. I had a hard time seeing and had to depend on Black Star.

I was traveling at a good five or six miles an hour, well ahead of Oteg, on a lagoon formed by the Innoko River, when the trail began to tremble. At once I realized that we were on ice, thin ice, no more than a couple of inches thick. Ahead of us it was billowing like waves on the sea.

Black Star saw the billows, too, and stopped the dogs. If we went on, the whole team, all of us, would go crashing down into the rushing river. We couldn't turn and go back because now the ice behind us had started to billow.

We were trapped. Panic seized me. I took a deep breath and tried to calm myself.

Black Star stood with his ears curled back tight against his head. He was trying to decide where to go, to the right or to the left. I was of no help. I didn't know what to do. It was Black Star's decision.

At last he turned to the left, toward a line of trees that marked the shore. He went slowly and the team followed him.

The ice grew thinner. It creaked beneath the weight of the sled. I got off the runners and walked to lighten the heavy load.

We went along toward the trees. Through the ice I could see fish swimming and blue water racing over the rocks. Black Star seemed to be sure where he was going. His head was up and his ears alert, his bushy tail curved high over his back. The rest of the team were dragging their tails. Every few steps they wanted to stop.

We were close to the shore now, but the ice was

thinner and full of bubbles. Suddenly Black Star pulled up. He glanced in both directions, trying to decide where best to make for the shore. The willow trees that marked it ran in a straight line.

After a moment he moved ahead in the same direction we had been going. Slowly he gathered speed, then, with the bank only a few yards away, he made a dash and scrambled safely to shore. The next five dogs followed him. Then the ice broke and the rest of the team fell through into the swirling water. The sled went with them and I went with the sled.

Dazed and blinded, I held tight to the handlebar. The dogs were struggling against the current, their heads up and silent. There was a gray mist among the trees, but I had a glimpse of my leader. He and his five dogs were pulling on the towline. With all my strength, I shouted, "Go, Black Star, go!"

The dogs clawed their way out of the water and up the bank. The sled got caught on a willow root. All of the team was pulling now and we were able to get the sled free. I staked the dogs out among the willows, built a fire in the cooker, and fed them some thick soup.

I was a sheet of ice, shivering and blue with cold. It took me a long time to peel off my frozen clothes and get into warm ones. I sat down by the cooker and was half thawed out when Oteg came racing through the trees.

"I saw your tracks," he said. "You took a wrong turn. You went right instead of left."

I remembered now that he had told me to go left.

"You lost an hour," he said.

"I forgot."

"Too bad."

He set out a pan of snow to boil for water.

"From here to Anvik," he said, "we will be going through a forest. Only one trail to Anvik. It is a narrow trail. Crooked, too. We go slow, huh?"

He made himself a pot of tea.

I started to harness the dogs.

"You better sleep before you go," he said. "You need sharp eyes on the Anvik trail."

I harnessed the dogs and packed the sled. Oteg was drinking his bitter tea when I left.

The night was still. The forest was close on both sides. I felt as if I were traveling in the darkest tunnel. All the trees looked the same. They stood up tall and straight like soldiers. Then the soldiers melted together. I was driving between two high walls. I looked up but saw no stars. I began to nod.

I got off the sled and trotted to wake myself up. There were some teams ahead of me, so the trail was packed hard. My boots made weird sounds on the hard snow.

The team was running better than ten miles an hour. They were glad to be out of the river and dry again. I grew tired at that pace and got back on the sled, which slowed the team down by half.

We left the forest and were now in open country, with far-off hills on the horizon and a moon. A strong headwind was blowing, but the temperature was well above zero. I took off my parka and gloves and opened my sweater. Still I was warm.

The slick runners made whispering sounds. The dogs ran together in long, loping strides. They made scarcely a sound in the snow. They were tired. I didn't push them. The moon and the hills became a hazy blur.

I began to nod once more. I was drifting down a broad river filled with salmon. Their golden scales glittered in the moonlight. They were leaping out of the water. They were trying to tell me something — one word over and over.

The dream suddenly faded. Again I was on a sled, moving through the night. I glanced over my shoulder. A team had slipped up behind me. The musher's lamp sent out a blinking glare. It was Oteg.

"Trail!" he shouted. "Trail!"

I pulled my dogs over and let him pass.

"I have followed Bright Dawn for two miles," he said as he went by. "She slept like a babe. But we do not sleep on the trail. If we do sleep, we may never wake up."

He hadn't yet congratulated me on winning the

$2,000. He cracked his long reindeer whip and was gone. He left a snowy mist in the night. His head-lamp glowed far down the trail in streaks of yellow gold.

At last, I thought, he has set me free to race my own race. It felt good to be free, but lonesome, too, and scary.

# 14

I came to Eagle Island at seven the next morning, just as faint light showed on the horizon. It was fifty-three degrees below zero with a sharp wind blowing out of the north.

The marshal said that it was warmer at Kaltag, the next checkpoint. So I went on for an hour, made camp, fed the dogs, and ate two chunks of muktuk. The whale fat and skin have a good flavor but take a lot of chewing. I got everything out of the sled, crawled into my sleeping bag, pulled the sled cover over myself, and set my alarm clock for noon.

Oteg woke me before noon. He came creeping into camp with three injured dogs and his leader dead. Two of the dogs he carried in the basket and one limped along behind him. The rest of the team looked beaten. Oteg, too. He had a bloody cut across his chin and one of his hands was bandaged.

I got out of my sleeping bag as fast as I could.

"Moose," he said before I could ask him what had happened. "Oteg is a lucky man to be alive."

"I saw three of them soon after I left Grayling."

"By the cave?"

"Yes."

"I saw three moose grazing close around the cave, but it was a good place. I saw a candy wrapper and knew you had camped there."

"A litter bug."

"I went to sleep. When I woke up, one of the moose was standing right over me, staring with its red-streaked eyes. I did not move. I barely took a breath. The moose walked away a few steps.

"My gun was in the sled, ten or twelve feet away. I did not get up. I rolled a little toward the sled. The moose walked back and stood over me again. A terrible thought came to me. I was going to die there in the snow. Killed by a moose."

Oteg had a hand wrapped in a piece of dirty cloth. His fingers, which stuck out, had turned blue in the cold. He tried to get a mitten on the hand, but it wouldn't fit over the bandage. He used his teeth and bit through the bandage and put the mitten on.

"The moose hung over me," Oteg said. "His lumpy snout hung down close to my face. I feared he was going to stay there until I froze to death. Then he grunted and walked off, not far.

"He kept watching. Another moose came up and

both of them watched me. Then they went over to where the team was staked out. The dogs were barking and trying to pull up their stakes.

"I lay very quiet. The beasts quit watching. They were curious about the dogs. I crawled to the sled and found the gun. It was in a bag and it took me a while to get it out.

"My leader had pulled up his stake. He was between the two moose. I heard a terrible sound. He was moaning. A sharp hoof had slit his throat. The other dogs were staked down, but they were trying to fight off the two moose.

"My first bullet struck an antler and whizzed back close to my head. The second bullet struck one of the moose square in the heart. The other moose came at me. The third bullet stopped him."

"I'll take your injured dogs to Kaltag."

"You will lose time."

"I will take time."

I made room for the dead leader and the three injured dogs and covered them with the sleeping bag.

Oteg said, "Leave them at Kaltag. And do not wait for me. You're in a race."

My team was anxious to go. Black Star was lunging at his harness. I hung back, hating to leave my friend.

Oteg said again, "Do not wait. This is the time to go fast."

I shouted, "Hike!" and pushed on the sled. Black Star lunged away. I looked back. The light from Oteg's lamp grew faint and faded away.

A half hour after midnight I got to Kaltag. After I checked in, I gave Oteg's dogs to the veterinarian. They were not seriously hurt, he told me, but they couldn't pull a sled. The dead leader we buried.

Word had come from Mr. Weiss in Ikuma. He had sent it that day by radio to the marshal in Kaltag.

"Mr. Weiss," the marshal told me, "said that the town of Ikuma asks God to speed you on to victory."

"Victory!" I exclaimed. "Is that what Mr. Weiss said?"

"That's what he said. Victory. I heard it clearly."

In less than an hour I was back on the sled. I found a place to camp and slept until dawn. Snow was falling. There were no dogs in sight when I woke up, only little round holes. They were buried in the snow and were breathing through the holes. I went back to sleep until ten that morning.

At noon, eight drivers left Kaltag in staggered order. In the lead was a girl I had talked to in Shageluk, who had advised me not to stand around at the checkpoints and jabber. Despite everything, I was running ninth.

A wind came up and drove the snow. Black Star forced the team to fight it. We moved through half darkness all day.

At four the next morning I camped off the trail in a small meadow protected by a ring of spruce trees. Wind roared through the tops of the trees, though it was quiet and peaceful on the ground.

I staked out the dogs, all except Black Star, who curled up at my feet beside the fire I had built. I dozed for a while and woke up to strange sounds. It wasn't the wind. I had heard the sounds before.

By now it was dawn. Orange and green light streaked down through the trees. I made out a wolf pack standing at the edge of the meadow. The leader took a few cautious steps toward the fire, then turned away. But before he disappeared I had a very clear picture of him.

From the brief glimpses I had had of him, all I knew about him was his color. In the dawn light I saw that his body was exactly the same pure white as Black Star's. Their faces were the same also. Ice-blue eyes that slanted up at the corners. Shadowy, foxlike masks around the slanted eyes. The black, starlike blaze on the foreheads.

The only difference between the dogs was that Black Star was younger by three or four years. Yet surely they came from the same family.

94

I remembered that Black Star's father was brought to our village by a trapper from Baffin Bay and mated to a Siberian husky. Suddenly it struck me that Black Star was the son of this wolf.

As the leader moved away from us, my dogs yelping at his heels, Black Star did not move. But his ears were pricked up, his body was tense, and his gaze followed the white wolf. Something had passed between them — a scent, a look, a sound I had not heard.

I needed sleep, two hours at least. I took my time and tied Black Star securely to the sled, then got into the sled and my sleeping bag.

I slept longer than I had planned and woke up covered with a blanket of ice. The snow had stopped, but the wind still roared. I took hold of Black Star's rope and shouted, "Let's go!" The rope came loose in my hand. The end was ragged. It had been gnawed through. Black Star was gone.

I jumped off the sled and cast a wild look around the meadow. It shimmered in the morning light. Footprints were everywhere — about the sled, the meadow, out of the meadow to the trail. Black Star and six of my team were nowhere in sight. But their tracks showed clear. They led north toward Ikuma and Nome.

Stunned, I harnessed the six dogs left to me. There was a chance, a small chance, that I could overtake my fleeing dogs. Running with the wolves, they would travel at a slow pace, hunting for food. Possibly, once the urge to join his father had been satisfied, Black Star would return. What the other dogs, the ones Mr. Weiss had purchased, would do, I didn't know.

The sun was lost in a bank of somber clouds. The clouds broke up into horsetails, the wind shifted to the east, and a heavy wind struck us. The dogs struggled against it, but we hadn't gone far, without Black Star to lead us, when they turned their backs to the wind and curled up in the snow.

With some effort I got them off the trail and into a stand of trees. I built a fire, fed them, and changed their boots. I ate the last of my ice cream and lay down by the fire.

I dozed for an hour and woke to find Black Star stretched out beside me, fast asleep. He always slept with one eye open, so in a moment he raised up and rubbed his cold nose against mine to beg my pardon for his absence. Then he curled up again.

# 15

The next checkpoint was Ikuma. My things were strewn about on the sled, thrown in any old way. I took time and put everything in order.

I changed my clothes from the skin out and put on sealskin pants and my best parka and the parka cover I had made of red cotton cloth. It had a flowery print of roses and looked like a summer dress. It matched the ribbon on the dogs' boots and the ribbon in my hair.

Now, when I drove down the main street, I would not be taken for a derelict. Now I felt like a racer. Black Star did, too. He kept pointing his nose toward the north, lunging at the towline. But there was one very bad thing. I had left Ikuma two weeks earlier with fourteen dogs. Now I had only seven.

A bitter wind sprang up. It didn't come out of the sky. The sky was clear. It came sneaking along the trail in angry gusts, driving icy arrows before it. I couldn't see through my goggles, so I took them off.

The dogs bowed their heads against the arrows. The sleet piled up and hid the trail. I walked out in front with Black Star to help him find the way. Then the arrows began to unravel the dogs' boots. In an hour of travel I stopped three times to take off torn boots and tie on new ones.

Yet, as the storm ended, one of my dogs was lame and I had to put him on the sleigh. I also had to change all their boots and clean the ice balls from their ears and eyes.

With myself there was nothing I could do. The parka cover was still in one piece, but it no longer looked like a summery dress. My hair was matted. My face, with all its spots and windburn, felt like a mask made of wood. Iron wood. But I couldn't lose more time. Now I was driving a team of only six dogs.

Faintly, in the distance, I saw a golden glow. Ikuma calls itself a town, but it's really a village and has no streetlights. Yet the glow came from there. The glow grew brighter, then as dawn came it disappeared and I saw blue smoke rising from the hill beside the village. They had built a bonfire to guide me during the night.

We went into Ikuma at a slow trot. Black Star strained at his harness and wanted to go faster, but the dogs behind him were tired.

The whole village was gathered on Main Street, which was two blocks long. The people were in the middle of the street. They formed a lane that was just wide enough for us to get through. It was like driving through a tunnel.

My friends touched me as I went by. My school-mates shouted my name. Amalia Yux and Sadie Tellon ran out and kissed me.

At the end of the tunnel Mr. Weiss and Mr. Gibson were waiting. They stretched out their arms, but before I reached them my father rushed out. He lifted me off the sleigh and hugged me until I could scarcely breathe.

My mother waited behind him. She was crying with happiness. Tears ran down her red cheeks. She had been cooking for a long time, getting food ready for me.

The town had built a platform in front of the Empire Café and draped it with flags and clusters of balloons. The school band was playing "God Bless America" with all its might. Mr. Weiss and Mr. Gibson stepped up on the platform with their wives, who wore ribbons across their chests that read BRIGHT DAWN in large letters.

I was too tired to enjoy the excitement. I almost forgot to check in. My father helped me up the platform ladder and went off to see about the dogs.

I needed to lie down and sleep, but Mr. Weiss

gave a speech and I had to listen, or at least to look as though I were listening. Then he asked me to give a speech. I don't remember the speech. I believe I said "Thanks" several times and that was my speech.

A crowd had gathered around the sled. They were petting the dogs, feeding them hamburgers and candy. The crowd followed me home, running along and singing beside the sled.

My mother had cooked a huge meal of fish soup and roast turkey, ptarmigan, and sourdough bread. I ate some of it just to please her, then I fell into bed and slept for three hours and dreamed that I was back in the cave with the wolves. When I woke up, Mr. Gibson and Mr. Weiss were talking to my father.

"She has only seven dogs left," my father said.

"Bad," Frank Gibson said. "Bad."

"And Blizzard has a crack in one of his forepaws. He can drop out anytime," my father said.

Mr. Weiss was troubled. "With a long way to go."

Frank Gibson was pacing the floor, pulling at his pointed beard. "The crack is an inch long," he said. "The dog won't last another day."

I was not troubled about Blizzard. He was a loafer, but tough. He would never give up. I drifted back to sleep.

The wind woke me up. It was thrashing against

the house, making weird sounds in the trees. It had blown the snow from the window and I could see Mr. Gibson and Mr. Weiss outside, walking among the dogs.

My mother said, "It is foolish for you to go in this storm. Not one driver has gone. I have watched."

My father got me on my feet. "Now is the time. Like your mother said, not one driver has left town. Not even the leader, as far as I know, has left. They're asleep and will sleep until daybreak. By then you'll be far out on the trail."

Mr. Weiss and Mr. Gibson had come in and were warming themselves at the stove. They were covered with sleet.

"I agree with your father," Mr. Weiss said. "Now is the time to go."

"This is the break," Frank Gibson said.

"A big break," my father said.

My mother was making thick caribou sandwiches for me to take.

Mr. Weiss said, "How do you feel, my girl?" He laughed and was very happy. Frank Gibson had quit pulling at his pointed beard. He was happy, too. "You look fine," Mr. Weiss said. "How do you feel?"

I was still asleep. "Fine," I said. My voice sounded like someone else's voice.

"The team is ready to go," Frank Gibson said. "We fed them fish snacks. Looked at their boots. Put salve on Blizzard's paw and wrapped it up."

"They're rarin' to go," Mr. Weiss said.

This wasn't true. When I pulled up the snow anchor, straddled the runners, and shouted "Hike!" Black Star was slow to move. He turned his head against the driving wind and started off crabwise.

The sky was black. The wind blew hard and steady. I went against it, zigzagging down Main Street, which was deserted. But there was something odd about the way the team pulled.

I stopped the team and went out along the towline. Nothing was wrong with Black Star. He just didn't like the wind. I patted Blizzard on the head and rumpled his ears. He was all right. Moon was all right, too. But next to her was a new dog.

The dog's body was white and it had dark spots on its face. I recognized it as a dog that belonged to Frank Gibson. He had put my team number on it and painted a slash mark on its back. The dog was meant to be a substitute for Blizzard if Blizzard had to quit the race.

A fresh dog would be a big help, now that I was down to seven and one of them lame. But I didn't wrestle with my conscience. To add a dog to a team anywhere on the trail was against the rules.

It took me a long time to get Frank Gibson's dog

unhitched and tied to the door of the Empire Café. The blizzard was blowing stronger than before. It was hard to see. A woman ran out of her house and gave me a sack of food. I didn't know who she was.

"Good luck," she called out.

I was tempted to go home and wait for daylight.

At the checkpoint, the race judge advised me not to leave. "You'll not get far," he said. "It's twenty below here at the cabin and the wind's blowing at ten. That makes the temperature somewhere close to thirty below."

"It was much colder at Kaltag," I said.

"You can lose a finger or two or a hand, a foot, and maybe your life," the judge said. He was doing his best to discourage me.

"I used to live near here, at Womengo. I know the country."

"If you can't see it, how will you know where you are?"

"My lead dog will know," I said.

We headed into the storm. Black Star would go a few steps and stop. I got off the runners and walked beside him, but he didn't want to go faster. Finally, I went out in front of him. Traveling this way, we made only two miles in an hour, which was very slow. My breath froze as soon as it left my lips.

Before dawn I stopped and fed the dogs a hot

103

meal from the cooker. I ate three of the sandwiches my mother had made and some of the bag of *peep-se*, the dried fish that the woman who ran out in the storm had given me.

I needed to sleep, at least for an hour, as did the dogs. We were blocking the trail, and though there was little chance that any of the drivers would come along before daylight, I thought it best to camp.

By chance I found a path that led off the trail. It was marked by fresh tracks, so many and so mixed up that I wasn't sure what animals had made them. They could be the tracks of fox or wolverines or even wolves.

At the end of the path was a deserted cabin. Its walls stood, but the roof had fallen in. Over the door hung the locked horns of two caribou bulls that had fought and died in battle. In my headlamp they showed a ghostly white.

I staked the dogs close to the porch and made a fire in a rusty iron drum out of wood that was lying about. The cabin door fell off when I opened it, and this I added to the fire.

After I had warmed myself a little I put my sleeping bag inside the doorway, out of the storm, set the clock ticking in my head for the hour of daybreak, and lay down to sleep.

I had not closed my eyes when a wolf came to

the doorway, hesitated for a moment, then leaped over my body and crossed the room.

In the glow from the fire I saw a nest of puppies lying in a corner. I watched while she chewed up a snow rabbit and fed them.

Wolves, if they aren't in danger, can be friendly, more affectionate than dogs. Yet she was a member of a pack, a pack that might return at any time and cause trouble. She might even belong to the wolf pack that had followed us, though I doubted this.

Fighting sleep and bitter cold, I thought about what I should do. The wolf's eyes glowed yellow in the firelight. While she nursed her pups, she watched me.

Overcome by sleep, I must have dozed, for when I saw her next she was sniffing at my hood. I lay still and spoke to her in the wolf talk I used with Black Star.

She answered me in the same tones. The tones rose and fell. They were wild, not even close to being human, yet as clear to me as spoken words. She had accepted me. She trusted me not to harm her pups. With one leap she disappeared through the doorway.

# 16

I went to sleep. My clock awakened me exactly at thirty minutes past three. The cabin was dark. I put on my headlamp and went outside. I tied a new harness on Black Star, changed boots on all the dogs, and started off. The trail had a light covering of snow over the ice, which made the sled easier to pull.

The storm ended slowly as we left the checkpoint at Unalakleet and a warm south wind sprang up. I began to nod. I pushed back my hood and untied my hair, but I still felt drowsy.

I got off the sled and ran behind the dogs. They were going too fast for me so I got back on the sled. I recited a poem I had learned at school and I counted backward, starting from the number 1,000.

It happened when I reached number 465. We were going through a spruce grove. A branch I didn't see struck me across the face and knocked me off the sled. The fall woke me up in time to shout "Whoa!" before the team disappeared. I had a cut on my nose and a bad headache. After that I didn't feel drowsy at all.

At Shaktoolik, the next checkpoint, the trail crossed Norton Sound to the checkpoint at Koyuk. I knew this treacherous stretch of sea ice. It was here that my father had nearly lost his life.

The blizzard blew away during the night, but as I got ready to leave, the headlands and the icy stretch of the Sound had disappeared. I couldn't see in any direction. I could scarcely see my own feet. A heavy white mist, like shredded cotton, had drifted in during the night and blotted out the world.

The three other drivers at Shaktoolik waited for the sun to come up. They thought that it would burn away the mist.

I knew better. Whiteouts could last for days. I was now running third behind the girl from Willow Creek. We were less than two hundred miles from Nome. This was my big chance to catch her.

I fed the dogs, changed their boots, and drove away an hour before dawn. The ice was covered with thin snow, which made the sled easy to pull. The dogs were in high spirits, their bushy tails curled over their backs. They wanted to go fast but

I held them back. It was a long way across Norton Sound.

After daybreak the air began to glitter like diamonds. White shadows swirled around us. One minute they were houses in a big village, then bare cliffs, then sailing boats on the sea, then trees and snowy mountains. I got dizzy watching them come and fade away, so I stopped and camped for an hour.

When we started up again and had gone about two miles, Black Star came to a halt and set his legs as if he had come to a cliff. I got off the sled and went out to see what was wrong.

As far as I could tell, the trail had not changed. So I walked on for a few steps to make sure we were not heading for a crack in the ice or open water. Black Star wouldn't have stopped had he not felt danger of some sort. He could smell danger half a mile away.

I had walked ahead farther than I thought, and when I turned back I couldn't find my footsteps. The trail I had followed only a moment before had disappeared.

I stopped dead still. I faced in what I thought was the direction I had come from. It seemed wrong. Then I faced in the opposite direction, toward the coast and Koyuk. But this also seemed wrong.

There was nothing to see except swirling curtains of white cotton. There was no sky above me, no ice beneath my feet. An awful thought seized me. It took my breath away. I was lost.

I had learned that the first thing to do if you are lost in a whiteout is to be calm. I had heard this from many hunters. In childhood I had heard it from my father. "Calm yourself," he had said. "And do not move. In an hour or two the whiteout will go away. And you are alive. You have not wandered off and fallen through a hole in the ice."

I listened for the dogs' barking. All I heard was a loud silence. Threads of cotton were pressing against my eyes. It was hard to breathe.

I sat down and put an ear against the ice. Sometimes you can hear noises from far off in this way. I hoped that drivers might be coming from Shaktoolik. I listened until my ear was numb. I heard nothing.

After an hour or so I heard a droning sound high above me. The sound grew louder and slowly died away. It could have been the plane that carried mail between Nome and Anchorage. When I lived in Womengo, it went over our house three times every week. If it was the mail plane, what direction was it flying? Northeast to Nome or southwest to Anchorage? I couldn't tell which way by just the sound.

I sat down on the ice and waited for one of the

drivers to come by. My sled blocked the trail. The drivers would have to go around it and my dogs would surely bark. They couldn't be more than a hundred feet away, but in what direction? I didn't dare move lest I wander off and go deeper into the swirling mist.

The sun was somewhere overhead when Black Star began to bark. I heard no sounds of another team. Probably the race was frozen because of the whiteout, as it had been frozen at Rainy Pass because of the blizzard.

The barking kept up. It was close, yet it came from all directions at once. I cupped my hands and shouted. My voice struck an icy wall and bounced back at me.

There was a short silence, then suddenly, as though they were floating in a white wave, Black Star and my team appeared. I grasped the handlebar as he swung the sled around and started for the trail. When he came to the trail he didn't stop, as he had before, but turned back toward Shaktoolik.

I shouted at him and tried my best to turn him around toward the checkpoint at Koyuk, but Black Star had sensed a danger in that direction. It could only be open water. The ice had broken up and destroyed the trail. He was fleeing from danger. He went fast, his nose close to the trail.

We had not gone far when, again, he stopped suddenly. Again the team piled up on him. I straightened them out as I picked my way forward to where he stood. His front feet were set. His head was raised high and he was sniffing the air, turning from side to side.

I had brought a rope, which I tied to the towline. I went forward cautiously, holding the end of the rope, determined that I would not get lost a second time.

The trail in front of me had changed. It reared up one way, then another. I slipped and fell to my knees. My headlamp went out. A few steps beyond, the trail came to an end. Beyond its jagged edges I saw deep water through the mist. I had been cut off. I was on an island of drifting ice.

I couldn't move. I stood and gazed at the icy water. Through rents in the mist, I saw that the opening was about five feet wide. I could easily leap this distance and the dogs could also. But where would we be jumping? Was it another island adrift like the one we were on?

I tied the rope tightly around my waist. Hand over hand, I found the way back to my dogs. They were sitting calmly on their haunches, waiting to be fed, except for Black Star. He had his head raised and was sniffing the air. He sensed danger as much as I did. For a while I forgot the danger. I built a

111

fire and cooked the dogs a hot meal of blubber and fish.

At dusk the whiteout began to break up. The creeping shadows slowly disappeared.

When night came, scattered lights showed along the coast from the villages of Womengo and Ko-yuk. But I couldn't tell whether we were drifting toward them or eastward into the vast Bering Sea.

The night grew cold. There was no wood for fire, and I dared not use the fuel I had for the cooker. On both sides of us rose lofty *eewoonucks*. I found a place among them that gave us shelter from the wind. Around midnight, the coast was a dark line on the horizon. Still, I could not tell where we were drifting — or whether we were drifting at all.

A short time later I saw in the distance the light from a headlamp bobbing along. As it drew closer, I recognized the powerful beam and the greenish glow. It was a special headlamp. It belonged to the girl from Willow Creek.

Her light was steady. She had not come to the break in the ice. I tried to make my broken head-lamp work, to signal her that I was in distress, but I couldn't get the wires together in the dark.

I heard her steel runners skimming the ice. She was not far away and running fast. My dogs were silent, I don't know why. I cupped my hands and shouted into the darkness, but the wind was blowing against me and carried my voice away. She did not answer.

Suddenly she was running slower. She had seen open water and was being cautious. Then I heard a whip crack and her team ran fast again. The break in the ice had not destroyed the trail. She was safe, on the far side of the water, headed for Koyuk. The greenish light from her headlamp grew smaller and disappeared in the darkness.

I had lost my lead in the race. Soon afterward a stream of headlamps poured down the trail and disappeared. I counted thirty of them. It didn't seem to matter. As the ice rocked to the movement of the waves and the wind moaned among the *ee-woonucks,* I was in danger of losing my life.

# 17

At dawn everything became frightening and clear. A piece of ice no larger than a hundred strides in every direction had broken loose. It was close to shore and the main floe in Norton Sound.

Open water lay on all sides of us. We were on a small island drifting toward the Bering Sea. There was nothing to hold it back.

I tried to stay calm. I built a fire in the cooker and fed the dogs part of their food and ate some of my own. I untangled the wires in my headlamp, put them together so the lamp worked, cut up the sled covering, and made a rough flag. Then I climbed the highest of the *eewoonucks* and fastened it to a hand pole I carried on the sled so that drivers could see it from the trail.

The day dawned clear, but by the time I got the flag set a cold mist had drifted across the island. Now we were hidden from the trail.

114

I flashed my headlamp. More than a dozen drivers went past before nightfall. None of them saw my headlamp. More went past during the night.

Heavy seas slanted across the sound. Waves broke in foaming crests. They were bearing us away from the trail and the shore, into the sea.

I cooked a small meal for the dogs. They were not on the trail pulling a sled at ten miles an hour, so they didn't need full rations. They didn't need them, but they set up a howl nonetheless.

Black Star was the worst. He scolded me with various wolf sounds, the sounds that were stronger than words.

There were three days of food for the dogs. They could go without food for two weeks, even longer. For myself, I had some chocolate bars and a supply of caribou chunks. Since the meat would not thaw in this weather and fuel for the cooker was low, I would eat frozen caribou.

Water would not be a problem. A thick coating of snow lay on the ice, and this we could drink.

The danger was not from lack of food or water. We could survive on short rations — or on none at all — for weeks if we had to. Nor was it the weather. Here on Norton Sound, the big storms were always over by the middle of March. I knew this because I was born less than forty miles from where I was stranded now.

There was a greater danger than starving or dying of thirst or freezing to death. We were drifting quickly away from the shore. Every hour, the wind and tide bore us farther toward the Bering Sea. At any moment, if hot weather came, our island could break up and be washed away by the waves. Already the edges of the ice where the waves struck were honeycombed and streaked with yellow.

By tonight or surely by the next morning, when I didn't check in at Koyuk, a search party would be sent out to look for us. They would use the trail, if it had not broken up. They would see the makeshift flag.

How they would reach it, I didn't know. A half mile of open water stood between us and the trail. By morning it could be two times that distance. The searchers would have to return to Koyuk or Womengo and bring back canoes or a boat if they could find one.

The mist burned away before noon. The sky was a clear gray and cloudless. But in an hour a warm wind from the land began to blow, at first in stiff gusts. Then it settled down and blew with a high whining sound. Green waves built up and beat against the land side of the island.

The wind and waves pushed us steadily seaward. We moved faster now than we had since the island broke away.

116

Shortly before dark a new sound rose above the sounds of wind and wave. A bright red and blue spot glinted against the gray clouds. It was the mail plane from Anchorage on its way to Nome.

The plane was flying low, just beneath the bank of clouds. As it flew over us, it made a wide circle, dipped its wings, and flew on.

The pilot had seen the camp. He had seen the flags and the dogs. He would know that it was not a seal hunter's camp, for this was not sealing time. He would reach Nome in minutes and report us.

When night came, I fed the dogs and myself. I ate more than I had for days. Now I felt sure that someone would come for us that night or the next morning, surely.

I climbed the *eewoonucks* where the flag was and from time to time during the night flashed the headlamp. The batteries ran out and I put in new ones. The island rocked gently. Now and then a piece of ice would break off with a roar. But most of the night it moaned like a wounded animal.

At dawn a wind blew in from the land. Then it rained, and the water collected in pools and the pools made holes in the ice. My thermometer read nine degrees above freezing. It made the dogs with their heavy winter coats uncomfortable. They dug holes in the soft ice and slept most of the morning. I had nothing to feed them.

Through the rain I couldn't see Koyuk or Womengo, nothing except great pieces of ice that had broken loose from the coast and were floating out to sea. There were no signs of a search party.

Then, a little past noon, a small plane flew over and dropped a package of food. It contained fish for the dogs, sandwiches for me, and a scribbled note that said, "Help is on the way and will reach you this afternoon. Be of good cheer."

The rain stopped. The wind grew cold and the pools of water began to freeze. I climbed an *ee-woonuck* and watched until dusk. No one came.

I fed the dogs and ate the food the plane had dropped.

At nightfall I turned on my headlamp, set it high on the hill of ice, pointed it toward the coast, and waited. Stars came out. Then the stars disappeared in a shower of lights. The lights changed color, they blazed and faded away as if the sky itself were breathing.

It was while a silver sheen covered the ice and the water that I heard the sound. It was not the sound of ice breaking up nor waves striking the island. It was different. And it came not from where my headlamp was pointed but from somewhere behind me.

I got down from the hill and walked, carrying my headlamp. I heard nothing more for a time.

I stopped and listened. It was very quiet. I put on my headlamp and stumbled toward the far side of the island. The light shone on a boat run up on a shelf of ice. A short, stooped man stood beside the boat. I ran toward him and he grasped my hands.

"What are you doing here?" my father asked in a trembling voice. "This is no place for you to be."

I couldn't speak to him. I was safe. The dogs were safe. We would not drift out to sea to starve and die. Yet my thoughts were only with him. He had returned to the places he had fled in horror. He was a crippled, fearful man, yet he had come back to the dangerous waters. In the light of my headlamp I saw that his hooded face was a ghostly white.

We were silent for a while. The island had shifted. It was now tilted to one side. The ice made creaking sounds as waves broke over the edge where the boat was moored.

"We are losing time," my father said. "You're still in the race."

I had given up all thoughts of the race. "Three whole days were lost. More than forty drivers are ahead of me. Fifty, at least. I'm finished."

My father put on his mittens. He raised his hands and brought them down hard, one on the other. "You're not finished until you cross the finish line in Nome," he said.

# 18

My father's skiff was not meant for two grown people, a seven-foot sled, and seven dogs. But by daylight we were settled. I stretched out on the sled with two dogs beside me. The Sound was covered with cakes of floating ice, so he couldn't use the sail.

It was a long, cold journey to Womengo. We didn't get there until late in the afternoon.

Our home had changed in the two years we had been gone. The climbing rose that my mother protected every winter had died. Its dead tendrils spread out like long gray fingers. The window was boarded up tight. Moss grew in the cracks of the door.

The whole village came down the road. They brought food, more than I could eat in a month. They fed the dogs choice pieces of reindeer steak. They sang the gay songs they always sang when the sealers went out in the winter.

I was too excited to enjoy anything. All I wanted was to hitch up the dogs and leave for Koyuk.

Bartok said, "Come and sleep."

He took me up the path to the house and put his hand on the doorlatch. He fumbled with it. For a moment I thought it had stuck. But it hadn't. He was struggling with himself. He was gathering courage to enter the home he had fled. I opened the door and we walked in together.

I slept for an hour. Then I woke up, feeling sleepier than when I lay down.

The big stove was gone. But Bartok had built a fire on the hearthstones and was sitting beside it, working on my towline, which had been cut by sharp rocks on the trail.

"If your line breaks on a hill, you're in trouble," he said. "And there are two bad hills between here and Koyuk, one going out of here."

He was using strands from an old tow rope. It was the same one that I had hung across the room the day he was lost among the *eewoonucks*. It must have reminded him of that terrible time.

He fumbled with the tow rope. It's hard to work with rope when you have only six fingers altogether.

"You liked the school in Ikuma?" he asked.

"Oh, yes." This was the first time he had talked about my school.

121

"Better than the old school in Womengo?"

"They were different," I said. "I had more friends in Womengo."

"Eskimo friends?"

"Yes."

"In Ikuma you have more white friends. In Ikuma your teachers were white, too. You are beginning to speak like them. You used to speak Eskimo. Now you don't anymore. To me, right now, you are speaking like a white girl."

He got up and put wood on the fire. He stared around at the empty room, the bare floor, the bare walls, the boarded window.

"The climber has gone," he said. "The rose I gave your mother for her birthday once. I never did like it. The catalogue said it was red and it turned out pink."

They had lit torches outside and the light came through cracks in the door. They shouted for me to come out.

"I like Eskimo talk," Bartok said. "White talk goes along smooth like a racing sled on an icy trail. Then there's a big loud bump that jars the teeth in your mouth."

"This English is hard to learn," I said. "Words like 'write' and 'right' sound the same but aren't. I still think in Eskimo. Then I translate the Eskimo words into English. My teacher wants me to learn to think in English first and not have to translate."

122

Bartok frowned. "If that happens you will be a white girl, not an Eskimo girl. This, I do not like much. What are you now, Eskimo or white? One thing or the other?"

"Eskimo," I said, to please him.

"Good! I am glad to hear you speak this way."

Out in the yard the singing stopped. Now everyone was shouting.

Bartok's eyes gleamed in the firelight. "It is good to hear Eskimo sounds again."

My friends were impatient. They wanted me on the sled, not talking, not eating, not sleeping, but racing to Nome.

Bartok held the towline and examined it foot by foot. He put out the fire and we went outside. He ran up the road and returned with an iron bar. He pried the boards from the window and carefully put them away in the house. He scoured the village and found a sled and five dogs.

"There's no trail from here to Koyuk," he said. "I'll make one. A good one."

It was snowing now, big fat flakes that floated down through the dark night like white butterflies. The village blazed with torches. Whale oil smoke hung in the air. Everyone cheered as we moved out of Womengo. Bartok led with a heavy twelve-foot sled that was used to carry water in the summer. It made a good trail through the knee-deep snow.

Koyuk was nearly eighty miles away.

The snow stopped before midnight, then sea fog crept in and Bartok had trouble making a trail. He had been traveling by sights on the North Star. Now he had to guess where he was going. The dogs were slipping on punchy snow, snow that was mostly ice. We stopped twice to dig it out of their paws.

Bartok went to his sled, got his deerskin pouch, and took out a bear's claw. It was curved and yellow and big. I had seen it many times before. For some reason, he had forgotten to carry the claw the time he got lost on the ice.

He held it out. "I leave you at Koyuk. Carry it to Nome. It will protect you."

I hesitated to take the charm.

"Take it," my father said.

I still hesitated.

A surprising look came into his eyes. "I see you don't believe in charms anymore."

"Not like I used to. Sometimes . . ."

"You can't be a half believer. Charms have no power unless you put true belief in them. I am sad that you have lost your faith while going to the white school," he said accusingly.

He closed his hand on the charm. I took it from him and hid it inside my parka.

"That's where it belongs," my father said.

I did not answer as we headed for Koyuk.

Koyuk is a small fishing village. Everyone

seemed glad the drivers had gone and that they had the place to themselves at last. But some of the schoolchildren came out to greet us. It had turned warm, about twenty degrees. They brought jugs of ice water to cool us and the dogs. Sled dogs need lots of water.

A little girl in a flowery summer dress appeared while I was checking in and gave me a candy bar wrapped in a ribbon.

"I hope you win," she said.

"Next year, maybe," I said, trying to smile.

"This year," my father said and shouted to the dogs.

They were well rested after the slow pace from Womengo. He swung his long whip over their ears. They pulled up the anchor and bounced away. I had to run hard to catch them.

"Do not forget the claw of the mighty bear!" my father shouted.

"I'll remember," I shouted back.

In answer, his long deerskin whip cracked in the wind.

# 19

The third hour we made only one mile. A fierce north wind held us back. There were thin clouds that didn't move in the sky and pale sunlight along the horizon.

Here below, a ground storm built up. It was filled with icy splinters, so many I couldn't see through my goggles. The dogs couldn't see. I had to stop and let them wipe their faces. While they were busy with their paws, I made snacks and fed them a lot of melted snow.

The ground storm beat us for two more hours. We scarcely moved. We came to a place where the trail branched right and left. The marker had fallen and was covered with snow. There were no sled tracks on either of the trails.

I decided to go to the left and after several miles saw a light. It was the light from a trapper's cabin. The trapper came out and hailed me.

"End of the trail," he said. "You should have gone right, not left. But welcome. Come in and I'll fry you a beaver tail."

He was a giant of a man with freckles, a red beard, and a squint.

"Thank you, but I'm in a hurry," I told him.

"Had dozens of mushers drop by the last few days. Took the wrong trail, just like you did."

"Why don't you fix the marker out there? Then they won't take the wrong trail and bother you."

"No bother at all. I get lonesome. It's good to have people to talk to."

He disappeared into the cabin and returned with a platter of sourdough pancakes two inches thick and a jug of honey. I ate one of the cakes and gave the rest to the dogs.

"How far is it to Nome?" I asked him.

"Most of forty miles. You'd best come in and wait for daylight. Trail's bad for a mile or two."

"Thank you, but I'm in a hurry."

"Shouldn't be. You're near to last. Enjoy yourself. Come in and talk. I'll tell you some fancy tales you never heard."

I thanked him and spent some time waxing the runners. They were in good shape. Altogether, I had waxed them five times.

After the pancakes and honey, the dogs were ready to run. We stopped where the trail branched. I dug around in the snow, trying to find the marker. I wondered if the trapper had buried it on purpose.

While I was at this, a musher came along, a woman with a team of bedraggled dogs. Her hair was gray, sticking out in strings from under her hood. She was old enough to be my grandmother.

"Which way do we take?" she asked. "Or don't you know?"

I found the marker. I stuck it deep in the snow, pointed it to the right, and piled snow around it.

"Are you sure that's pointing the right way?" she asked.

"I'm sure," I said and began to tell her what had just happened to me, but before I could finish, she shouted to her dogs and was gone.

The trail was bumpy for a few miles. In the bad places I ran beside the sled, pedaled with one foot when the trail got better. The gray-haired woman was close in front of me. I caught glimpses of her headlamp bobbing along.

As the sun rose, a brush plane flew low over the trail. It was blue and glittered in the sunlight. Under the wings was a sign that read: WELCOME TO NOME! CONGRATULATIONS! WEISS AND GIBSON!

Congratulations on what? I was the last driver in the race, the very last.

The woman was less than a mile away. Her gray hair flew out behind like a banner. She had a whip in her hand. I heard the whip crack. I heard her shout, "Go, you hellions!"

I did not need to shout. Black Star didn't like to see a team in front of him any more than I did. He lunged against the towline. The whole team came alive.

We raced into Main Street. Black Star brought us even with the other sled. But at that moment he made a terrible mistake. As we were about to pass, he swerved in and gave the woman's leader a sharp nip on the ear.

We lost a second, two seconds. Not more than three. Yet that was enough. We sped under the Iditarod Arch just behind her, spattered with ice and slush from her sled.

# 20

I drove back to the finish line slowly. Flags hung down from the Iditarod Arch, faded and stiff in the cold. Under the arch stood my father and mother. Bill Weiss and Frank Gibson were wrapped in their parkas and their breaths hung frozen in the air.

Mr. Weiss had a bouquet of flowers in a box, but before he could give them to me, my mother had her arms around my shoulders. She was crying.

My father clapped his hands and acted as if I had come in first instead of last. Mr. Gibson said that he had engaged a room for me at the hotel so I could rest and dress up for the banquet.

The winner's banquet had been held already. The girl from Willow Creek had won the Iditarod and $50,000 of the $200,000 prize money. But a lot of people came to the banquet that night, more than a hundred. A woman official spoke a few words and gave me the two thousand silver dollars I had won for being the first musher to reach Iditarod.

But that wasn't all, not nearly. She handed me a check for $2,500. "This is the prize for winning the Sportsmanship Award," she said.

$2,500! I had never heard of the Sportsmanship Award.

"It is given for the best display of sportsmanship during the race," she said. "For going out of your way to help other mushers, even though it cost you time in the race. Ralph Stone, the checker at Kaltag, reported that you were helpful to a friend and his injured dogs. Ms. Jacobs reports that you took valuable time to find and put up a lost trail marker."

Then she handed me a red lantern, the kind that hangs on the back of a train's caboose. Everyone clapped their hands and laughed. I laughed, too, but not very much.

When I sat down, Mr. Weiss whispered across the table, "Don't forget that you finished the race. Thirty-six mushers out of the seventy-one who started didn't finish."

"I'm proud of the red lantern," I said and half believed it.

My father beamed. I didn't think he was surprised that I had finished. My mother grasped my hand under the table and held on to it. Later when we went back to the hotel, she asked me how I was going to spend all the money I had won.

"I haven't thought about it," I told her.

"We're going back to Womengo, your father and I. But I don't think you should go with us. You've graduated from high school. You've earned good grades. You love books. There's a fine college in Anchorage. You must go there and study."

This was all new to me. Never before, never since I had graduated from the school in Ikuma, had she said anything about my going on with my studies.

"What would I learn in Anchorage?" I asked her.

"To be a teacher."

"Teaching what?"

"Everything! Your marks are good. You can be a good teacher in any subject."

"That's what you always wanted to do," I said.

My mother's eyes clouded over. Was she thinking about the day her high school geography class had gone to Womengo on a field trip? The day she had first seen my father at the Trading Post, the morning he was telling one of his fanciful tales, the time when she had fallen in love with him, with his red cheeks, his broad shoulders, his rich, rumbling voice?

"You could come back to Norton Sound and

help our children," she said. "They're caught between two worlds, their own and the white world."

She paused, suddenly aware that I was still in the race, driving a team of sled dogs through the night, runners singing, my headlamp searching out an icy trail.

"You need to sleep," she said.

"For days," I said.

But next morning before the sun was up I was out with the dogs. I was too excited to sleep. I cooked them a meal of whale oil and fish. All of them except Black Star sniffed at it and turned away. I had made the mistake the night before of feeding them beefsteak scraps from the banquet. Black Star went down the line from pan to pan and nearly foundered himself. It was the only time I had ever seen him conclude that his stomach was full.

Mr. Weiss and Mr. Gibson gave a five-course breakfast for my family and me. I ate little of it. I was still on the trail. Mr. Weiss and Mr. Gibson talked about next year's Iditarod. I listened but said nothing.

After breakfast Mr. Weiss had the plane ready for us.

"Leave the dogs," he said. "There isn't enough room. The plane will pick them up tomorrow."

"I would rather take them back myself," I said.

133

My father and I harnessed up the team while my mother watched. We would meet again in Ikuma. Then we would pack two big sleds and take the trail back to Norton Sound and Womengo.

Our goodbyes were silent. The morning was clear with a brisk wind from the sea. The red lantern was wrapped in a caribou robe. The silver dollars were packed in a big wooden barrel. The $2,500 check I carried in my parka, fastened to the lining with a safety pin.

I felt richer than I ever thought I would be. I was happy that my father was going back to Womengo and the sea he had fled. But most of all I was happy about myself. I was not the same person who had left Ikuma long weeks ago. How I was different, I didn't know. But it was there, deep inside of me.

The trail had a thin coating of snow. The sun was warm. I wanted to take my time and see the river and the hills I had only glanced at before, but Black Star was full of fire, so I shouted "Go!" and let him run with his tail straight out and his ears pinned back, scooping snow as he ran.